The Light

from

the Dark

To Anja and Odma

For helping me make this what it is

To my sweet family

For all of your love and support

Table of Contents

Forlag: Books on Demand GmbH, København, Danmark

Tryk: Books on Demand GmbH, Norderstedt, Tyskland

ISBN: 9788743012825

The Opportunity

Adriana Carter stared out the east-facing window of her small apartment, taking a few moments to enjoy the colorful sky which heralded the arising sun. Her short, black robe was cinched loosely, and the cup of coffee in her hand was already half empty.

As she gazed out at the rolling green hills, at the winding streets that seemed to fold into one another, and the present stillness of the town square, she could almost forget why she was there.

She had arrived a little over three months ago, and the time had both flown and dragged.

Adriana had been a support professional with the Federal Bureau of Investigation for four years, and she had enjoyed her work immensely, more than she had expected when she first started. The dream had been to be a curator but, as those jobs were becoming fewer and fewer between and she had rent to pay, Adriana decided to put her education towards a more practical and sustainable profession. Her specialty had been in identifying counterfeits, whether it was art, or money, or passports. She had been highly regarded by her peers and was considered to be quite the star.

That was, until the day that it all came crashing down.

There had been five suspects, whose identity were in question. Adriana had closely examined each and every passport the men had been using as proof of their claimed identity and had deemed them legit. They had been released later that day.

A week later, another case led agents back to the five men, and it turned out they were part of a terrorist sleeper cell, and all five had been on the terror watch list.

Adriana was devastated and the guilt ran rampant. She was the reason they had been released in the first place and it was only by chance they were caught again, before they could do anything deadly.

When Adriana was called into her boss's office, the first thing she did was to lay her badge on his desk. She was shocked by what had happened next.

"Sit down, Carter." Jacob Wentworth barked. "Don't be so quick about turning that over."

She took a seat immediately but it took a few moments before she could speak. "What are you talking about, Sir?"

He gave her an irritated look. "Did I mumble?" Wentworth went on without waiting for a reply. "You fucked up big time, no one can deny that."

Adriana had opened her mouth to protest but realized there was no defense good enough.

"If it were up to me, you'd already be being escorted from the building but, as it turns out, it seems you can be of some use to another department. Go see Grant Marks and get the hell out of my sight!"

Grant Marks headed up a team that had been investigating organized crime. Throughout the course of the investigation, a person of high interest had emerged in the form of a suspected Italian criminal mastermind named Agostino Gismondi.

All official channels they had tried to use to connect the man to the circuit in the US had led to dead ends.

To that day, she was still somewhat baffled by what had been presented to her.

Marks knew that the person of interest was an art aficionado and figured that the least suspicious cover would be one posing as an art dealer.

As luck would have it, in addition to her degree in art history, Adriana spoke fluent Italian as well. She had always felt drawn to the language and grabbed onto the opportunity to study it at an advanced level, when she was at university.

Marks had told her it would require going in with minimal contact and essentially no cover. He did advise her, though, it would be for the best not to mention the FBI in any way, shape, or form, but to build upon the work she had had, before she started with them.

If she succeeded in making an irrefutable connection between the man in Italy and the crimes in the US, she would be welcomed back with a clean slate.

Adriana had readily agreed, despite her lack of intensive field training. She was so amazed at being given a second chance, that she did not question it so much.

That was how she ended up in Italy. She had been set up with a small, but sufficient apartment, and space for a small gallery and enough paintings to make it functional. The monthly stipend she got was enough to cover the basic expenses and afforded her the lifestyle of a fairly successful art dealer. A contact of Marks' had arranged the residency papers. After that it was just a matter of playing the waiting game and looking for an opening.

The last bits of coffee were finished, and she set the cup on the ever-growing pile. There were few things she hated doing more than dishes, so it tended to pile up, until she absolutely could not avoid it anymore.

Adriana made her way to the bathroom and began the ever-tedious process of getting ready. She had always been more of a wash-and-go sort of girl, but it did not take her long to realize that certain appearances must be kept, *bella figura* as the locals would say, so she endured the ritual every morning. Adriana always took the time to review what she had read of the alleged crimes Agostino Gismondi was at the very least associated with. She had not been allowed to have any physical nor digital records so she had to keep her memory sharp.

Her dark brown, wavy hair, which fell past her shoulders, was gathered up into a high ponytail. She scrubbed her face clean, then smoothed foundation over it. Her skin was nice and taut, her only being twenty-nine years old.

Tito Cavello-penis and testicles crudely cut off. The wounds had been cauterized. Cause of death: gangrene, complicated by sepsis; most likely, a rusty knife had been used to remove his genitals

The eyeshadow came next, a combination of colors that made her light-brown eyes pop. After a brief battle with the eyeliner, eye lashes were curled and mascara applied.

Fiorello Ongaro-Cause of death: heroin overdose. No previous track marks found. High probability of being a forced overdose. Signs that he had been sodomized with an object prior to his death

Her lips she saved for last, lining them, smearing on the lipstick, followed by a dab of gloss. She examined her reflection carefully, only being satisfied when no blemishes were found.

Enrico Locatelli-beaten from head to toe.
Numerous broken bones, some teeth ripped out, small
cuts up and down his arms and legs. Cause of death:
massive internal bleeding

Her hair took almost as long, with all of the
brushing, fluffing, teasing, and spraying that was
involved. She tweaked it until every last strand was in
place, making sure it covered the birthmark on the side
of her neck. There were many days she wished she
could just run a brush through it and be done with it,
but she knew those days would not be for a while.

Money laundering, bribery, extortion

Adriana walked the few steps required to get from
the bathroom to the bedroom, discarding her robe on
the way. She reached into her closet, grabbing
whatever appealed to her first. The undergarments and
dress came on in quick succession. The dress was
fairly loose but it clung in all the right places. She
stood just around one hundred and seventy centimeters,
with long legs and a willowy frame.

Tax evasion, forgery, insider trading

Her feet slipped into the trendiest pair of black
heels, and she surveyed herself from head to toe,
pleased when everything seemed to be as it should.

The shoes made loud, clacking sounds that she
briefly hoped did not bother her downstairs neighbor.
Her smart phone, cigarettes, lighter, and keys were

6

tossed haphazardly into her purse, and she grabbed the giant thermos of coffee that was waiting on the counter before slipping out the door.

It was only a five-minute walk from her apartment to the gallery. She cut through the square, which had begun to show signs of life now that the sun was fully up in the sky.

Adriana turned the key in the lock and automatically disarmed the alarm system, her fingers knowing the motion. She settled down at the small table and took out her phone, opening the latest game to while away the time.

She would have the occasional customer every now and then, but it was not the one she sought. Still, Adriana played her part because she knew, in a town like this, reputation was everything and if she shot that, she would have no chance of making contact with him, and any hope of redemption would be lost.

Some days she was sorely tempted to try to initiate contact, but Marks had warned her against that. He said the man spooked easily and a sure way to arouse his suspicions would be to act aggressively.

Adriana was snapped out of her thoughts at the tinkling of the bell, and when her eyes wandered over to the door, she saw a tall man in his late-thirties, with dark, wavy hair, a goatee, and chocolate eyes. He wore a tailored suit and a friendly expression on his handsome face.

"*Buongiorno!*" Adriana called warmly, immediately rising and making her way over to the man. He returned her greeting in kind. "How can I help you, today?" Her Italian was nearly as fluid as her native tongue.

"I'm looking for a painting for a gift. Papà is quite partial to the Romantic period. Do you have any such paintings like that?"

"I do indeed. Please, come with me." She led him over to a wall. "Does he have any particular favorite painter?"

The man gifted her with a pleasant smile. "He has always said he cares little for the name and more for the art itself."

Adriana returned the smile. "Your father is a wise man." She pointed out a painting, which hung on the far side of the wall. It was a scenic piece of a dirt path that was surrounded by tall trees, buds of green and white adorning the branches, the starts of flowers popping up from swaying green grass, all leading to a clear blue sky. "He might enjoy this piece. The artist is up and coming but has a solid grasp on the Romantic concept. It's entitled 'Spring has Sprung'." When she said the words, she saw something flick across the man's face, but just as quickly, it was gone. She was not even sure she had not been imagining things.

He studied the painting closely, examining the distribution of the color, the shading, the ease of the brushstrokes. When he stepped back and looked past the painting, Adriana knew it was almost sold. If he was going so far as to envision it on a different wall, he was seriously considering it.

His gaze wandered over to Adriana, and it rested just a couple of beats too long. When he realized this, he threw on a disarming smile. "I'll take it."

She was slightly surprised. He had not even asked how much it cost, much less haggled over it. "It is priced at one thousand Euros," she said doing her best to keep her tone neutral.

"And it is worth every cent!" He replied with a laugh.

Adriana merely nodded and smiled as she took the painting down. As she was preparing it, the man asked her a question.

"Do you do appraising work by chance? I know Papà mentioned the other day that his insurance company wishes to have some of his paintings reappraised, but his normal consultant is on holiday. He has quite a few paintings and was looking for one to come out to the house one day. Is it something you would be interested in doing?"

"Of course! I'm always happy to help out a customer." She began filling out the receipt form on her laptop. "May I have you name, please?"

"Macario…Macario Gismondi."

Adriana felt her heart skip a beat, but she wanted to be sure. "Is your father Agostino Gismondi?" She did her best to keep her face even, not daring to hope she was finally getting an in with the man who would unknowingly be her path to redemption, until she was absolutely positive.

Macario nodded. "One and the same."

Her mind was racing with this latest development, so much so that she nearly forgot to introduce herself. She cringed and laughed nervously. "I'm so sorry. I don't know where my manners disappeared to today! I'm Adriana Carter. It is a pleasure to meet you." She extended her hand, wanting to kick herself. First impressions lasted around here and she would hate herself if this particular chance was shot down before it even took flight, because it was very unlikely that she would get another.

Macario took her hand and when he held it his grip was not firm, but tight. His eyes met hers for several long seconds. "The pleasure is all mine."

Adriana was not sure what to make of the whole thing. There was definitely no flirtation vibe coming from him. It was more like a tender affection, even though that made little sense to her. She brushed the thought away, merely relieved she had not completely offended him.

10

"I'm sure Papà will be just as charmed as I am by you. Do you drive?"

"I'm afraid I do not. I've always found it to be a bit intimidating." While she did know how to drive, Marks had told her she would have to cover car expenses herself and she did not think it was worth the trouble. She did not, however, want to explain that to Macario, so Adriana opted for the little fib.

Macario responded with a kind smile. "Yes, a good deal of the time it is often crazy versus crazier. Let me check with Papà and see when the best time for you to come by would be. I'd be happy to drive you out there myself."

"Oh, I'd hate to be a bother! I can just take a taxi. I really don't want to trouble anyone."

"It is no trouble," Macario insisted. He glanced at the receipt and confirmed that the phone number was the correct one. After that, he picked up the packaged painting and gave her one last smile. "I will be in touch, soon."

She smiled in return and waited until the door had shut behind him before sharply exhaling. She was still in a state of almost disbelief, that the long-awaited opportunity had finally presented itself.

It took the better part of half an hour to calm herself, but Adriana finally managed it. All of her willpower was required to not stare at her phone, willing it to ring. The ball was finally rolling.

The Appraisal

Adriana had hardly been able to sleep the night before. Macario had luckily not kept her waiting. He had called less than an hour after he departed, and asked if she could possibly come by the next day, to which she had gladly agreed.

After the initial exultation, reality started to sink in. She had been told by Marks in explicit detail how dangerous a man Agostino Gismondi was. The smallest slip could give everything away, and her only hope would be any mercy he might have.

Despite her initial concerns, Adriana was now quite grateful that she had no cover story. The nerves were making it hard enough to remember her own past. She genuinely doubted that she could keep a fake history straight.

Getting ready was a longer endeavor than normal, as she had to keep stopping to calm her shaking hands. She knew she had to pull herself together, otherwise her behavior might as well be a red, neon sign that she was up to something.

Macario was not due to arrive at the gallery for another twenty minutes, but Adriana was too anxious to sit in her apartment, so she went out. She hoped the fresh air would do her some good.

She was not sure if it was two or three cigarettes she had smoked, but it was finally enough to get her to act like a normal human being. She pondered lighting another one, just to be sure, when she saw Macario walking towards her.

They greeted each other warmly, and he yet again gave her that odd handshake. After a short bit of polite chit chat, he led her in the direction of his car.

Macario gave her a warm smile. "May I ask how long it's been since you arrived in Italy?"

Adriana cringed, yet there was a smile on her face. "Is my pronunciation that bad?"

"On the contrary! One could say you were born to speak Italian." He cleared his throat before continuing. "I can hear a slight accent, but it is not pronounced enough to pinpoint where you are from."

She was surprised to feel her heart swell a bit at his compliments. Her cheeks felt a bit warmer than normal as she avoided his gaze, hoping he would take it for modesty. She had to remind herself that she could not feel friendly towards him, not if her mission was going to succeed. "I moved here a little over three months ago, from the US. I decided to finally make proper use out my university education."

"I hope you have found our little town to be a welcoming place."

"Of course! Everyone has been very friendly."

"I'm very happy to hear that. I would hate to think we were giving a bad impression!"

Adriana lightly laughed. "There is no concern for that, don't worry."

"Papà really appreciates you being able to come by on such short notice."

"It is my pleasure." She was starting to worry that she had seemed too eager, had accepted too quickly. After all, she made no mention about having to close the gallery for a whole day. Adriana tried to assure herself that nothing of Macario's behavior was indicating that.

They reached his car, a black Maserati Quattroporte S Q4. She did her best to not let her eyes bulge. It was only a few occasions she had ever been in that close of proximity to something so luxurious.

Macario followed her to the passenger side and opened the door for her.

"*Grazie*," she said with a smile, sliding into the seat. A quick glance around told her everything was top of the line. *Forget sitting in the lap of luxury…I'm enveloped in it,* she thought to herself as Macario went around the back of the car.

When he turned the key in the ignition, the engine purred to life. He cast a brief glance around before pulling out onto the road.

Adriana did her best to cover the nervous gasp, but she did not succeed.

Macario laughed a bit. "My apologies. For what it is worth, I promise we will reach Papà's house safe and sound."

Adriana replied with a smile, though she still maintained an iron grip on the door handle. She was beginning to be thankful Marks had decided a car for her was not in the budget.

The narrow streets soon gave way to a country road, as they headed northeast. Her grip on the handle started to relax a bit as she took in the splendid scenery.

"It is a beautiful place, no?"

Adriana nodded as they swept past sycamores, Swiss pines, and maples, the car hugging every curve. It was obvious Macario had driven the road countless times with the way he handled every twist and turn automatically.

The day was clear and bright, bringing a special life to the occasional vineyard they passed, as the road climbed higher and higher.

After fifteen minutes, Macario turned off the road, stopping in front of wrought iron gate. He reached out the window and pressed a button. A few moments later, the two halves of the gate began to slide to either side. As soon as it was wide enough, Macario's foot was pressing down on the accelerator, and they shot up the long driveway, tall trees and perfectly manicured grounds on either side.

Adriana's eyes widened when they got past the shield of trees. She had heard plenty about the villa but never had she imagined anything like this. The pale brick walls towered over almost everything, with more windows than she could estimate at a glance. There was a marble staircase that narrowed as it ascended, leading to the main door. Flowers of all colors and shrubbery ran from one end of the house to the other. There was even a large fountain bubbling away by the stairs. She was so lost in the marvel of it all that she barely noticed Macario signaling her to wait.

He went around the car at a brisk walk, opening the passenger door once again and extended his hand to Adriana.

She put her hand in his and tried to shake her mind back to reality and to the matters at hand. Focus was required and she could not be distracted by grandeur.

As they headed towards the steps, Signore Gismondi emerged from the villa, raising his hand in greeting. He stood tall, several centimeters above one hundred and eighty, and his medium build seemed as solid as it had been in the prime of his youth. His once wavy, dark hair had turned a silvery gray but was still thick upon his head. Lines streaked his face, but his light-brown eyes had not lost any of their sharpness. His age did not stop the powerful feeling he exuded, though. If anything, it added to it. He was dressed impeccably; a dark pinstripe suit which had been tailored specially for him, and shoes, which had been polished to a shine.

Adriana felt her heart speed up when their eyes met one another. She was finally seeing the living, breathing version of all those files she had read. She attributed that fact to the sense of familiarity she felt towards him. That was the only logical explanation.

"Papà!" Macario gave his father a quick embrace. He motioned towards Adriana. "Your fellow art lover has finally arrived."

She thought it rather odd that Macario had not used her name, but perhaps he had found it unnecessary, given that it was obvious who she was. Adriana extended her hand towards Signore Gismondi and was slightly surprised when he clasped it with both of his.

"It is a pleasure." Signore Gismondi gave her a warm smile. "Thank you for coming by on such short notice."

She forced an easy smile. "The pleasure is all mine, Signore." She had decided to say nothing in particular in regards to the short notice part. From all of the information she had read, a request from Signore

Gismondi was more like a command, which could not be ignored under any circumstances.

When he released her hand, he stretched his arm out in the direction of the steps. "Please, come in."

Adriana ascended the stairs, with Signore Gismondi by her side, and stepped in. She tried to not choke when her eyes took in the interior. The arched ceiling stood high, an elaborate crystal chandelier hanging from the center. The wide staircase swept up and to the left, covered with a plush carpet. Exquisite paintings adorned the walls and sculptures could be found in every corner. She managed to compose herself, remembering that high class clients were supposed to be her specialty.

"Your home is so beautiful, Signore Gismondi!"

Signore Gismondi briefly bowed his head. "I am glad to hear you think so."

Macario, who had been hanging back, stepped towards the two. He caught Adriana's gaze with his own. "May I ask how long you estimate you will be? I only ask because I have a few errands to tend to."

"Well that all depends on how many pieces there are to examine." She turned towards Signore Gismondi.

"There are five in all. Though I had been hoping I could persuade you to join me for lunch. The paintings are but one of the splendid things I love to share!" His smile shined as bright as dawn.

Though she was nervous about the idea of being alone with him for so long, Adriana saw this as a chance to snoop out some things, so she plastered on a smile. The food she had brought could always be eaten at another point. "I would be honored to, Signore Gismondi."

Macario gave a quick nod. "I shall return in the afternoon then." He gave his father another embrace and Adriana noted him whispering something in Signore Gismondi's ear, though she could not make out what. Macario took Adriana's hand in his again, before heading out the door.

When Macario had made his exit, Signore Gismondi turned to Adriana. "I must tell you, the painting you picked out has become one of my favorites. You have remarkable tastes."

Adriana feigned bashfulness. "I must say, Signore Gismondi that is quite the compliment, coming from one such as yourself!"

There was a flicker of something in his light-brown eyes that Adriana could not quite place.

He led the way down a long hallway. Paintings and photographs lined the walls, each frame of the highest quality. The way they were all spaced and arranged was nothing short of museum quality. She tried to take it all in, certain that everything that adorned the walls were originals.

Adriana followed him into a large room. There were bookcases that ran the length of the room on each side, the same height as the room, and they were filled to the brim with books. A sofa and several large, plush chairs were placed into the center, along with a table and a couple of chairs to the side, as well as a large desk, but that was not what took her breath away.

On the opposite end of the room, rather than a wall, glass ran from the floor to the ceiling. Adriana could make out a doorframe, but it was subtle enough that it did not distract from the panoramic view. A couple of dozen rows of grape vines were what she spotted first, then olive trees to the right of them. The rolling hills stretched further than her eyes could reach, and the late morning sun poured into the room.

"Signore Gismondi, this is exquisite!"

His smile beamed. "This has been the favorite room of everyone in the family." After a brief pause, he continued. "This room has the best natural lighting. I thought that was best for your work."

"You are absolutely right, Signore."

"The paintings are laid out on the table over here." Adriana fell into step with him and gave each painting a quick glance. There was one of sunlight streaming through the leaves of a weeping willow, which was nestled by a small pond, one of a harbor at sunset, one of a windswept field, one of a night sky filled with constellations. The final one was strikingly different from the others. It was a dining table, complete with nine place settings and chairs. Adriana was quite curious about it but decided to save that for last.

"Do you have everything you need?"

"Almost." She pulled her laptop out and placed it on the table. "If possible, I'd like to log on to your WiFi. I'll be needing to reference catalogues as part of the process."

"That is no trouble at all. My youngest son is educated in the IT business, and he made quite the complicated password when he set the network up, so it'll just be easier for me to type it in myself." He turned the laptop towards him and bent down ever so slightly.

Adriana played with the idea of seeing what other computers she could connect with through the network but decided that could wait, for the time being at least. She gave him a smile when he straightened up again.

"I'll just be out on the patio. If there is anything you need, please, let me know."

Adriana nodded and waited until he had stepped outside before prepping for the work ahead. The first thing she did was to fish an elastic out of her bag. She drew the sides of her hair up and secured them to keep distracting hair from falling in her eyes. A notebook and several pens came next, which she set next to the first painting. The magnifying glass was the last thing she took up. When all was arranged to her liking, Adriana slipped on a pair of thin, white satin gloves to avoid skin oil transfer to what, she had no doubt, would be very valuable pieces.

She began with the painting of the weeping willow. The first thing she did was to hold the magnifying glass over the small monogram in the lower right corner. A small "F" was set in the open space of a large "D", and Adriana immediately recognized the mark of Fabrizio Donati. Upon thorough inspection, she could say with confidence that the mark was genuine. Assured that it was not a forgery, she continued with the rest of the appraisal.

Adriana held the magnifying glass over the upper left corner of the oil painting. She intensely studied the glazes, how they blended together, and noted the faintest pencil lines almost hidden underneath the light-colored paint. She moved the magnifying glass a few centimeters to the right and investigated that area and continued the process until she reached the other end. She started once more, directly beneath the spot she had begun. Adriana repeated the system until every last centimeter of the painting had been examined. There was enough variation in the brush strokes to assure her that it was an original rather than a highly advanced print. She picked out a couple of spots that showed her conclusion and took a picture over the magnifying glass.

The next step was to look at the painting as a whole. There was incredible depth to it, enough to give one a sense of being able to step right into the painting and be in that moment, something she remembered Donati being very well known for. There was a sense of softness to it as well, which demonstrated the high skill of the painter.

She then turned her focus to the frame. It was made of solid, dark wood with intricate carvings in the corners. When she went to lift it, she was pleased, but not surprised, to find it to be on the heavy side. That was another check for the value of the painting.

A couple of gallery labels were affixed to the back of the canvas. Adriana noted the names, intending to check their records. If they matched, it had gone through the proper channels and was a legitimate purchase, rather than something that was obtained through the black market or the like.

Satisfied with all the evidence, Adriana proceeded to the next step . She removed the gloves and sat down in front of her laptop. She found a catalogue that included Donati's works. Apparently, the piece Signore Gismondi had was one of his earlier works.

Looking at recent auction house sales for other Donati paintings, she was able to conclude a value of 7,500 Euro for that particular painting. She started making notes, documenting the steps she went through, and how she had come to the conclusion she did. Adriana knew insurance companies and auction houses liked that sort of thing.

She had just started typing, when she heard a light knock at the door. Before she could say anything, the door opened and an older, petite woman stepped into the room, greeting her with a smile.

"I'm very sorry if I am disturbing you, Signorina. My name is Marie. I am Signore Gismondi's maid."

Adriana greeted her warmly, though she felt a bit awkward at the extreme courtesy Marie was showing her. "You're not disturbing me at all!"

"I am happy to hear that. Is there anything I could get for you? Some coffee, or water, or something to eat?"

"Yes, please. Some coffee would be lovely."

"I'll bring some right away." She gave a quick curtsey and slipped out of the room, before Adriana could so much as blink.

Adriana became distracted from her appraising work, as she considered a more indirect way to get what she needed. Servants tended to know a great deal about the happenings of their employers. Perhaps there was a chance she could get Marie to flip on Signore

Gismondi. She pushed the thought to the back of her mind, for the time being.

It was a short time later that Marie came back into the room, the cup of espresso on a tray. She set the cup to the left of the laptop and gave Adriana a warm smile and turned around to leave.

Before she could think about it, Adriana spoke. "Marie, would you mind if I ask you a question?"

Marie quickly turned to look at Adriana. "Not at all, Signorina!"

Adriana tried to make her voice as casual as she could. "How long have you been working for Signore Gismondi?"

There was a great deal of pride in Marie's face and voice. "I've been with the Gismondi's for nearly forty years."

Adriana's eyes grew large. She was not sure why but that was a lot longer than she had been expecting. "That is very impressive!"

"The Gismondi's have made it easy. They treat me like family. I couldn't ask for better."

She accepted the fact that her brilliant thought was anything but. Adriana could clearly see Marie would never turn on any of the Gismondi's. She gave Marie a warm smile. "Thank you for answering. I was just... curious."

"You're welcome, Signorina." Marie once more gave her quick curtsey and made her way out of the room.

Adriana stifled a sigh and took a sip of the coffee. She turned her attention back to the report, not wanting to displease Signore Gismondi and having that door shut on her as well.

It was roughly an hour that had passed from start to finish on the first appraisal. She rolled her neck, a satisfied sigh escaping her lips when she heard a delightful pop. Adriana decided that a little break was in order, and she fished her cigarettes and lighter from her purse. She made way for the door, which had been propped open.

Her heels made soft clicks as she stepped out onto the patio. Signore Gismondi was sitting a couple dozen meters away, by the table next to a large pool. He was talking on the phone, but he still raised his hand in greeting.

Adriana gave a small wave back before she turned slightly, to give him some privacy. She became slightly nervous. After all, they had never discussed breaks. She could only hope that he would find it permissible. There was a small table to her right, with a crystal ashtray sitting on it. She lit the cigarette, taking a long drag from it as she let her eyes clear from the first painting. She was so wrapped up in herself and her thoughts that she did not notice Signore Gismondi approaching.

"How is it going?"

Adriana hid her slight jump and turned towards him with a smile. "It's going very well. I've finished the Donati piece. I'm going to get started on the Oscuro piece next. I've just found that it is best to take a little break in between each painting." She did not entirely succeed in masking the slight nervousness in her voice.

"I completely understand! When it comes to art, one's eyes are the most important tool. A piece can lose half its meaning, if even a small part is overlooked."

Adriana smiled softly, momentarily forgetting just who he was, and just relieved she had not upset him. "I couldn't have said it better myself, Signore." She crushed the end of her cigarette in the ashtray. If she was honest with herself, Adriana almost felt like she was defiling the crystal. She gave Signore Gismondi a kind look. "I should head back inside now and continue the work."

She got about one step before Signore Gismondi stopped her by clasping onto her shoulder. "Take as much time as you need. Good work cannot be rushed." He gave a soft squeeze. "Lunch will be in two hours' time." He turned and walked back towards his table.

Adriana took a moment to shake herself out. She was slightly weirded out by his behavior, but she tried to not let it distract her too much.

The Oscuro piece of the harbor at sunset took nearly as long as the Donati painting. Adriana took her eye break once more. She cast a glance to her left and saw that Signore Gismondi was not at the table. The thought did cross her mind to try to take a peek at the laptop sitting on the table, but then thought better of it. He could return at any second, and there was absolutely no reasonable explanation she could give. For a reason she could not describe, she had a feeling this would not be her only opportunity to gather information.

When she went to ash her cigarette, she noticed the ashtray had been emptied and cleaned. Adriana guessed Marie had been by. She considered telling her the ashtray did not need to be emptied every time but figured it would be kindly ignored. Besides, Adriana hated the thought of telling someone how to do their job.

The Zullo piece of the windswept field came next. The appraisal went a bit quicker, only due to the smaller size. Adriana was quite impressed with the level of detail in the painting. Each and every blade seemed to have a life of its own. She found it rather enchanting.

Adriana finished up the report and decided to take the time to reread the others. Just as she had read through the last report, Signore Gismondi walked in from the patio. "Lunch is ready."

She gave him a smile as she walked over to him. Showing Macario was not the only gentleman in the family, he allowed her to step through first. Adriana fell into step beside him as he led the way over to the table by the pool.

Two plates of bruschetta had already been placed on the table, along with two glasses of rosé wine. Signore Gismondi pulled Adriana's chair out for her before he took his own seat. He gestured towards her plate. *"Buon appetito."*

"Grazie." Adriana replied with a smile. She took a delicate bite and her taste buds were woken in a most delicious fashion. There was no doubt, to her, that there was a vegetable garden in another part of the grounds, and the tomatoes had been picked and chopped just before being put on the crostini. Adriana managed to keep her face even though. While she was not supposed to have the sort of money that Signore Gismondi did, she should be used to being around people with his wealth and in getting tastes of their everyday life. *"Delizioso!"*

Signore Gismondi replied with a bow of his head. "All credit goes to my chef, Giuseppe. He's been with us for almost thirty years now, and he has never once disappointed."

Adriana raised her eyebrows in an impressed fashion. She wondered how a man, who was supposed to be as cold and cruel and corrupt as Signore Gismondi, could command such loyalty from his staff. Perhaps, the prospect of a steady paycheck made Marie and Giuseppe look the other way. Perhaps, they knew nothing about his doings. She hoped, she could one day find out just what it was.

"May I ask how much progress you've made on the appraisals?"

"Of course! I've completed the work on the Donati, Oscuro and Zullo pieces so far. I'll be starting on the Sabbatini piece after lunch and working on the Li Fonti piece last."

Signore Gismondi gave her a cryptic smile. "Which is your favorite piece, so far?"

"The Zullo." Adriana's answer was immediate. "Even the blades of grass in the background seem to have life to them. The way she has played with the lighting is both daring and ingenious! Even though you can't see the sky above, you have no trouble pinpointing where the clouds are, and what shapes they have!"

"I am quite partial to that one myself, for those exact reasons." He raised his wine glass towards her. "*Salute.*"

"Salute." Adriana replied, clinking her glass with his. The Bureau part of herself tried to ignore the fact that she had anything in common with a career criminal. She could barely stand the thought, even if it was over something as insignificant as an opinion on a painting.

A brief time after the two finished the bruschetta, Marie came out with an empty tray. Signore Gismondi gave her a warm smile as she collected the plates. She then collected the glasses, her thumb resting on the base of the one Adriana had drunk from. "Giuseppe will be out shortly with the primo."

"Grazie, Marie." When she departed, Signore Gismondi turned his attention back to Adriana. "Have you been enjoying the late summer we've been having?"

Adriana smiled. "Somewhat, yes. Though to be perfectly honest, I'm looking forward to autumn. Cooler but not cold is the perfect temperature, in my opinion. Mostly because I love any reason to put on a nice, warm sweater, but not have to go around with a jacket."

"So, red wine temperature?" His expression was amused.

Adriana lightly laughed. "Yes, I suppose that would be an appropriate description."

Giuseppe emerged from the house, bearing the same tray that Marie had had earlier. He seemed to be around the same age as Signore Gismondi, though he was on the plumper side, as any good chef should be. His demeanor was warm but with slight hints of formality as well. He gave a smile to the two sitting at the table. "*Buongiorno,* Signorina. I hope the antipasto was to your liking."

"Absolutely!" Adriana was slightly thrown that he was addressing her, rather than Signore Gismondi, but she quickly recovered from it. "I'm not sure I've ever had better!"

Giuseppe gave a brief bow. "I'm quite pleased to hear that. I can only hope you have the same sentiments with this dish." He set a plate of mushroom risotto, as well as a glass of red wine, in front of her, before doing the same for Signore Gismondi.

"*Grazie,* Giuseppe." Signore Gismondi said with a nod.

Giuseppe returned with a nod of his own before he tucked the tray under his arm and walked back into the house.

Adriana was somewhat surprised at the courtesy Signore Gismondi showed Marie and Giuseppe. She had thought for sure men like him would see thanking a servant as beneath them. While it was possible it was a show he was putting on for her, Adriana did not find the possibility likely. Why would he care if an art dealer thought him rude?

Signore Gismondi's voice pulled her out of her thoughts. "So, if you had to pick one favorite art movement throughout history, what would it be?"

There was no hesitation in Adriana's answer. "The Macchiaioli movement. It's actually what I got my master's degree in."

"There were some exquisite works that came out of that time."

"Odoardo Borrani was always a particular favorite of mine, regardless of movements."

"I must say, I've always found '*Donna con candela*' to be at once enchanting and disconcerting."

"I completely agree!" Adriana had managed to yet again completely forget whom she was talking to. "I've always been fascinated with it because even though it was painted in the nineteenth century, it is almost like a shot from a modern-day, psychological horror movie!" She paused to take a sip of wine. "His works just have so much range! If one were to look at '*Donna con candela*' and '*Vada vista da Castiglioncello*', they would probably never guess they were painted by the same artist!"

"Yes, and his paintings within the painting, such as in '*Visita allo studio*', are magnificent and give such life to each piece."

Adriana enthusiastically nodded. "There's such energy with so many of his pieces but some have such a sense of serenity to them, like with '*Giovane donna che culla il bambino*'."

Signore Gismondi's expression was wistful, with tinges of something that Adriana could not quite pinpoint. "Everyone can find a work they enjoy by him."

"I couldn't have said it better myself!" Adriana held her glass up and clinked hers with Signore Gismondi's when he did the same.

Giuseppe came out a short time later and swept the empty plates and empty glasses away, with the promise of being back shortly with the main course. She briefly thought it odd that it had switched from Marie to Giuseppe for the collecting of the dishes, but she chalked it up to Marie being busy with other duties.

"Do you enjoy literature as well?" Signore Gismondi inquired as they waited for Giuseppe's return.

"Work keeps me quite busy so I haven't had as much time to read as I'd like, but I do enjoy it. I have a list of classic novels that I'm slowly working through."

"Have you read *The Betrothed* by Alessandro Manzoni, yet?"

"A couple of times, yes. It's probably the reason I haven't made as much progress on my list as I'd like. I always seem to keep coming back to it."

"If there is anything in the library that interests you, you are more than welcome to it."

At that moment, Giuseppe came back out. He placed the plates and the wine glasses in the same order as last time. Adriana remembered to thank him as well.

"You are an extremely cultured young woman. It is very refreshing to see when so many of the younger generation seem to not have appreciation for the fine arts."

"Thank you." Adriana's reply was quieter than she had intended, while a dark memory flitted through her mind.

"If I'm to be perfectly honest with you, I think you'd be better off choosing another line of education." The middle-aged guidance counselor said with a tone completely devoid of enthusiasm.

"But, art is what makes me grin. It makes me feel energized in a way nothing else has ever done. I feel more passionate about it than anything else I have ever experienced. Why shouldn't I make it my life's work?" Adriana was nearly kicking herself. She should have

known the last meeting before the start of her senior year would take the course that it did.

"It's not too often that your sort get an opportunity like this."

She could feel the anger building up in her chest. It felt like someone had clamped two, unyielding boards to the front and the back of her. Adriana had learned long ago to keep her temper in check, but she found herself to be struggling like she never had before. "And what, exactly, do you mean by 'my sort'?"

The guidance counselor shifted in her seat, ever so slightly. "Those who have grown up in the system."

"Well, forgive my snideness, but I'd say that's more of a fault in the system, than it is to do with us. It's the choice of the adults to change the system. None of us chose to be born to parents who didn't give a shit about us!"

The counselor's eyes widened slightly, clearly not used to being challenged in such a decisive manner. "I'm just saying, you have an opportunity that is not easily gotten. I just think it is best that you don't let it go to waste."

She was still amazed at what came out of her mouth next. "Well, I guess you'd speak from experience about wasted opportunities. How else would you have ended up becoming a guidance counselor?"

Adriana did not even care when the meeting was cut short. She recounted the events to a couple of acquaintances at the group home when she returned. The grins she got from them was the most warmth she had gotten in the previous several months. Adriana had learned many a years ago to not let the indifference get to her. That was why she had clung to the fleeting moments, such as those.

That guidance counselor had not been the first, nor the last, whom had tried to tell her she should choose something more practical, something with more job security. While security in any form was something Adriana had craved her whole life, she knew her passion was too strong to deny. She held fast because she had fought for her excellent grades in high school, had fought to get into university, had fought to get her scholarships. What right did any of them have to tell her she should not do what she had fought tooth and nail for? When she did indeed have difficulty breaking into the New York art scene, she adapted and got her job at the Bureau. She had been tempted to, but ultimately resisted the urge, to go and gloat to each and every guidance counselor. "There was no shortage of people who tried to discourage me along the way. While I understand everybody has different passions, I think one of the biggest problems is the lack of support for those who want to enter the field. Of course, if more people took the fine arts more seriously, there would be less stigma for those who want to study and make a living out of it. I know uncertainty is terrifying, but there is no field where there is zero unemployment."

Signore Gismondi nodded, a cryptic expression on his face. "When one truly wants something, there is nothing that can stand in their way of getting it." He paused briefly. "I think the world of art should be grateful that you could not be dissuaded from your calling."

Adriana felt a blush creep into her cheeks. She knew she should not be as flattered as she was, but she could not help herself. Even her colleagues at the Bureau, while nice, would perpetually tease her, saying things like she should thank her lucky stars that six years of study were not completely wasted. She never let on just how much those comments bothered her. "I think that is one of the kindest things anyone has ever said to me."

His eyes were locked with hers. "I speak only the truth."

A shiver shot down Adriana's spine, as she noticed the intensity in his eyes. She was sharply brought back to reality and reminded of just whom she was sitting across from. She managed a small smile and distracted herself with the chicken breast with a mascarpone sauce.

When they finished with lunch, Adriana gave Signore Gismondi a kind smile. "Thank you very much for a lovely lunch, Signore."

"Thank you as well."

Adriana forced herself to keep her smile as she excused herself. Normally she would have enjoyed a cigarette after such a good meal, but she wanted a little distance between Signore Gismondi and herself, so she headed right back into the library.

She did as she had told Signore Gismondi she would and got to work on the Sabbatini constellation piece. Being the same size as the first two, the piece also took around an hour. Her need for nicotine finally won out and she headed out to the patio, hoping Signore Gismondi would let her be. Adriana relaxed considerably when she saw that the table was empty.

She was mostly frustrated with herself, for letting herself get charmed by him. Having her ego fed should be a non-factor for her and Adriana promised herself that she would not get swept up again.

Adriana began work on the Li Fonti piece with the table settings. She had briefly wondered why the artist had chosen the number nine specifically. As she was about to start the magnifying investigation, Adriana heard the door open and turned her head, expecting for it to be Marie.

Instead, Signore Gismondi and Macario walked through the door.

"*Buongiorno!*" She greeted the two warmly.

40

They returned the greeting in kind.

She looked at Macario. "I'm sorry, I'm not quite done yet. I shouldn't be much longer though."

Macario waved his hand. "Don't worry about it! Take your time. One of my children wants to borrow a book, so I wanted to get it before I could forget again! I'll never hear the end of it, if I do."

Adriana lightly laughed to mask the hurt she felt in her heart. To have a relationship with a parent like that is something she had accepted as never happening for her but, sometimes, she still hated that fact.

"We won't be disturbing you, will we?" Signore Gismondi asked.

She was slightly surprised he seemed to be asking her permission. "Absolutely not, Signore!"

"I'm glad to hear that." He gestured over to the bookshelf across from where she was working, and Macario followed him over there.

Adriana bent over the painting once more, while the Gismondi men talked quietly. There were five place settings on one side of the table and four on the other. Two chairs had a shawl each draped over them, the one to the right of the middle of the five chairs and one across from it. She was completely enchanted by the quality of the shawls. Adriana felt as if she could reach into the painting and pull them out. She was so taken up with what she was looking at, she forgot how self-conscious she was over her birthmark and swept her hair back over her shoulder. That was, until she heard the conversation between the Gismondi men heat up. She glanced up and when she did, she saw Macario had a firm grip on his father's arm and was trying to head for the door.

Neither had noticed Adriana watching them. "Come with me now, Papà." Macario's voice was low but firm.

"Is something the matter?" Adriana asked as nervousness built in her stomach, wondering what she could have possibly done wrong.

Both of their heads whipped over to her. Macario spoke before his father had the chance. "No, nothing's wrong at all." He tried to give her a reassuring smile. "There's just a matter I need to discuss with Papà.

"Okay." Adriana forced herself to turn back to the painting, trying to convince herself that Macario had spoken the truth. She watched Macario tug Signore Gismondi out of the room from the corner of her eye.

When the door shut, she finally let out the breath she had not noticed she had been holding. Both of them seemed so intense and she had no idea what could have suddenly prompted that. Adriana did her best to push the thought from her mind as she got back to work.

When she examined the back of the piece, she noticed a note about it being a commissioned piece. It seemed that Signore Gismondi had asked Li Fonti to make this particular painting. Adriana noted that it was truly one of a kind and adjusted her appraisal value accordingly. She finally noted her pushed back hair and hurriedly made to cover her birthmark again.

A half an hour passed and Adriana finished up the last report. She had done what she could for the day. She had a list of the galleries she needed to get in touch with to finalize the reports. Her things were packed down in her bag and she gave the paintings one, last appreciative look.

She was not sure where to head to so decided to wait out on the patio until somebody came by. It was shortly after she lit a cigarette that she heard someone step out and turned to find Macario lighting his own cigarette.

He gave her a warm smile and his demeanor gave no sign of what had transpired just before. "All done for the day?"

"As much as I can be. I'm sorry for keeping you waiting!"

Macario shook his head. "Think nothing of it! I've had a very open day today, so it is no trouble at all. Besides, it made me finally remember the book!"

Adriana softly laughed. "Just how many times have you forgotten it?"

"That you would have to ask my oldest son about! I'm sure he's documented each and every incidence." Macario finished up with a grimace. "In my defense though, he hasn't been especially good about remembering to ask for it when we've visited either!"

"I'm glad for you that the saga seems to finally be over." Adriana's expression was greatly amused.

Macario smiled in agreement. "Just let me know when you're ready to head back into town."

"Now would be fine for me, if that's alright with you."

Macario nodded. "Let's go find Papà." He led the way through the labyrinth, past the front door and coming to a stop. He knocked lightly on the partially open door. "We're going back to town now."

Signore Gismondi strode out of the room and stopped directly in front of Adriana. "It has been an absolute pleasure having you here, today." He clasped her hand in both of his.

"The pleasure has been all mine, Signore."

"Tell me, have you experienced a proper, homemade Italian dinner?"

"I'm afraid I have not had the opportunity yet."

"Then I insist you join us for dinner here tomorrow. I won't take no for an answer."

Adriana could hardly believe how quickly she was being accepted by him. With some luck, she would have what she needed by the month's end and she could return to her old life. She gifted him with a warm smile. "It would be an absolute privilege, Signore."

"Wonderful!" Signore Gismondi declared. "Macario," he waited until he had his son's full attention. "You'll pick her up around seven tomorrow evening?"

"Of course, Papà." The look he gave his father was one Adriana could not quite discern at that moment.

"Only if it is no trouble for you! I'm sure I can find a way out here if it is."

"There'll be no trouble at all. I promise." Macario responded warmly.

Adriana inclined her head in agreement. She bid Signore Gismondi farewell, before following Macario to his car. She did her best to keep the extra bounce out of her step.

The Family

Adriana had dug out her finest clothes, knowing only the best would be acceptable. The weather had changed overnight, the late summer slipping into a crisp autumn. The midnight blue, spaghetti strap, cocktail dress flowed and the soft, cream bolero sweater helped give a classic look. A pair of dark heels, studded with rhinestones, adorned her feet. The sides of her hair had been pinned up and the lower part curled around her neck.

She had only been able to keep the gallery open a couple of hours in the morning, her nerves getting the better of her as the day progressed. She used the extra time to make sure she looked flawless. If she ended up making a poor impression on one of his sons, Adriana had no doubt that they would have an easy time changing their father's opinion of her. She could not let this open door of opportunity slam shut in her face.

Macario was rather prompt in picking her up. After exchanging pleasantries, they began the drive to Signore Gismondi's mansion.

"I really do appreciate all the driving you've been doing, Macario." He had told her earlier to use first names in order to avoid great confusion later in the evening. While he had not said it, Adriana assumed that did not, also, include Signore Gismondi. "There must be something I can do. Perhaps pay for petrol or something of the like?"

"I meant what I said. It really is no trouble. My trips to and from Papà's are quite frequent, so this is nothing out of the norm for me. Well, with the exception of having some lovely company."

She gifted him with a smile. There was something about his behavior that she could not quite put her finger on and she felt slight knots in her stomach. Adriana tried to take a deep breath as subtlety as she could. If Macario noticed, he gave no indication.

The drive went quickly, partly due to it being her third trip in the past day and a half, and partly due to the way Macario drove.

When they arrived, Adriana spotted five other cars parked in front of the house. There was another Maserati, two Lamborghinis and two Ferraris. It was almost like a luxury car showroom. She did her best to not let it intimidate her.

The sun was on its way down when Macario helped her out of her seat and led her up to the door, opening it for her.

When Adriana stepped through, her eyes landed on Signore Gismondi, who had a beaming smile on his face. She did not even have time to bid him a good evening before he swept over to her and Macario.

"Welcome! Welcome!" Signore Gismondi graciously greeted them. He embraced his son, then turned his full attention on Adriana. When his hand met hers, rather than shaking it, his fingers curled around hers and he brought her hand up to his lips. "I'm so very happy to have you back. You look as beautiful as ever."

Adriana felt the blush creep into her cheeks and she tried not to become flustered. "Why, thank you, Signore. I very much appreciate the invitation." She held out a wrapped box of chocolates to him. Adriana had gone by the best handmade chocolatier in town, not wanting to scrimp on a host gift. While it was said the gift was of importance and not the price, she did not want to take any chances, even if it meant light lunches and dinners for a week.

Signore Gismondi looked like he was about to say something but became distracted when Macario cleared his throat. His gaze returned to Adriana and he gave her a dazzling smile. He took the gift and unwrapped it, his smile growing impossibly larger as he looked at the chocolate box. "My absolute favorite!" The shine in his eyes matched the brightness of his smile. "I have some things to tend to in the kitchen, but I promise you, we will be talking much more."

Adriana was slightly surprised that he wanted to oversee Giuseppe making the dinner, but she did not let it show on her face. "Of course."

"Macario, could you take her into your brothers?"

"Yes, Papà." Macario gestured to the right, while Signore Gismondi went down the hall to the left.

48

When they reached the sitting room, Adriana saw the five other Gismondi sons standing around, drinks in hand. Each was dressed in what she was certain was a tailored suit. She found herself hoping her little cocktail dress was acceptable enough.

"*Ciao!*" Macario called out and the others turned towards them.

Adriana's eyes moved from one to the other, not sure where to begin, if there was some sort of unofficial hierarchy.

"Allow me." Macario said, placing a reassuring hand on her shoulder.

"This is Valentino." Macario gestured to the second eldest of Signore Gismondi's sons.

Valentino was the tallest of them, and he was just as wide as he was tall. He was all muscle though, and Adriana would have found him incredibly intimidating, if not for the infectious smile on his face. She held her hand out to him. "Adriana Carter. It's a pleasure to meet you."

There was a flash of something across his face when he took her hand in his that Adriana did not have time to place, before Macario continued the introductions.

"This is Dante."

Dante was a middle brother in every way. Middle in build, middle in height, middle in temperament. His face was covered in stubble but Adriana had the hunch that he was one of those men who seemed to be perpetually sporting a five o'clock shadow, no matter the time of day.

Adriana did the same as she had with Valentino. She noted that there was a great deal of warmth in Dante's eyes.

"This is Constantin."

Constantin was of a height with Macario, but was clean shaven. She noted the two looked quite a bit alike, though not enough that they could be mistaken for twins. Constantin's hair was thick and slicked back and he seemed to have an incredible amount of energy.

As she shook his hand, he had the same type of grip Macario had. Perhaps he was more like his older brother in ways other than looks.

"This is Ignacio."

Ignacio was on the border between lanky and scrawny, with tight curls covering his head. His boisterousness made up for his lack of build.

There was a smile with extra warmth when he took Adriana's proffered hand.

"This is Sergio."

Sergio was the smallest of the brothers, though he still stood a few centimeters taller than Adriana, despite her high heels. He was the most reserved of them and gave her only cool politeness.

His handshake was brief and almost immediately after, he turned his back to her, helping himself to another drink. She hoped she did not do anything to offend him. Adriana tried to focus on the positive impression she made on the others.

"Would you like a drink?" Macario inquired.

"Yes, please. That would be lovely."

Macario poured her a glass of Prosecco, handing it to her before taking one for himself. He lifted his glass in the air. *"Salute."*

"Salute." Adriana replied with the others, clinking glasses and remembering to hold eye contact. The last thing she wanted to do was to start the night by activating a superstition.

"You arrived here three months ago from the States, right?" Dante questioned. When Adriana nodded her confirmation, he continued. "Where did you grow up?"

"New York State. I moved around a lot so there isn't a particular town I'd call home." That had always been her diplomatic way to describe the long string of foster homes that stretched back as far as she could remember.

"Did you attend university there?" Constantin asked.

"Yes, I did. I studied Art History. I got my Bachelor's from New York University and my Master's from Columbia University."

Valentino looked impressed. "Those are two excellent schools."

"Are you in the art field as well?"

"No, no I'm not. I work in finance. But Papà's passion has rubbed off on all of us, to greater and lesser degrees. Out of all of us boys, Ignacio is probably the closest who has made a career out of it."

Adriana turned towards Ignacio.

"I own an import/export business. It has a focus on designer items but the occasional painting can come through."

Adriana nodded, thinking how convenient that could be for Signore Gismondi, but not letting it show on her face. Perhaps Ignacio was one to keep an eye on. "Is it IG Imports?"

"Yes, that's the one."

"If you ever want to expand your gallery, just let me know." Constantin said. "I'm sure I can find you exactly the space you need."

Macario rolled his eyes. "Don't you ever not work, Constantin?"

Constantin gave his brother an incredulous look. "This coming from the family lawyer."

"So, what brought you to Northern Italy?" Sergio questioned. There was an indiscernible expression on his face.

"In addition to my Art History, I also studied Italian. Art can take on a whole new meaning when one can understand the title and the historical influences." She hoped she was being as charming as she was attempting to be. After the others indicated their agreement, she continued. "There was just something about the area, which I felt connected to. I could never quite put my finger on it, just that I felt there was something for me here." That part at least was true. It was part of why she had agreed to Marks' proposal without a second's hesitation.

Dante was the one to speak. "I think we all understand the sentiment."

Adriana gave him a smile. "I'd love to explore more of the country someday."

"Our mother was from Southern Italy." Macario said. There were traces of sadness on his face and in his eyes.

While Adriana was aware of Signore Gismondi being a widower from his file, she put on a surprised and sympathetic look. After all, Signore Gismondi had made no mention of his wife the day before. "Oh. I'm so sorry for your loss."

"So, what are your parents' names?" Adriana's classmate asked her.

"I don't know."

"You don't know? How could you not know?"

Her nine-year old self struggled to find an answer. "I never knew them."

"How could you ever not know your own parents?"

Adriana shrugged. "Something happened after I was born, so they're not around. No one could ever tell me exactly why. I've had a lot of different pretend parents, though."

"That's so weird!"

The only thing Adriana could think to do was nod.

"We lost her almost thirty years ago." Valentino told her.

"Still."

Out of the corner of her eye, Adriana saw Sergio fill his glass yet again. She took a sip of her own glass, trying to act like she had not noticed.

Signore Gismondi strolled into the room and it awed Adriana how he could command all attention to himself without as much as a word. "The antipasto is ready." He held his arm out to Adriana, waiting until he secured her arm in his own before turning and leading the group out of the room and towards the dining room.

While the room stretched long enough to hold several tables, there was one large one in the center of the room, directly under one of the several crystal chandeliers that hung from the high ceiling. Despite the large amount of space, there was an underlying sense of intimacy permeating the room.

There were eight place settings, four on each long side of the table. The appetizer plate was made of bone china and was painted with an intricate pattern in red, with a ring of gold along the edge. The wine glasses were long stemmed and glimmered thanks to the chandeliers that hung overhead. The silverware was polished to a shine. It was much finer than any restaurant she had ever been to, and she struggled a bit to not get swept up in all the grandeur. Adriana did have a job to do, after all.

Signore Gismondi led her over to her seat. Adriana gave him an appreciative smile, as he pulled her chair out for her. As the others took their spots, she realized she was seated to the right of Signore Gismondi, the place of honor. She tried to not think too much about it. After all, she was the only guest. The rest of them were family.

Macario was on Adriana's right and Sergio on Signore Gismondi's left. Valentino was across from Adriana, with Dante on his left and Constantin on his right. Ignacio was across from Sergio.

The antipasto had already been plated, but there were extras on the serving platters in the center of the table. There was bresaola with Grana Padano, Prosciutto di Parma with slices of Parmigiano Reggiano, and the Culatello di Zibello rested on slices of bread.

Signore Gismondi looked at each of his sons in turn, and Adriana got the distinct impression that making them wait was almost a game of his. His eyes rested on her, and he gave her a warm smile. *"Buon appetito!"*

The Gismondi sons needed no more prompting from their father and within seconds, they were all cutting into the antipasto.

Adriana tried to approach hers in a more delicate manner, and she kept mentally repeating what she could remember about dining etiquette. Wrists above the table at all times, do not switch the fork from the left to the right, wait until the host has taken a sip of

56

wine first. She had no desire to make a faux pas, especially in front of such a refined group. Adriana had always been intrigued with high society and had read up on manners and etiquette during her university years. She tried to reassure herself that her manners were at least passable.

The taste of clove from the bresaola was strong but not overpowering, the prosciutto had just the right amount of salt to it, and when she took a bite of the culatello, she understood why it was considered the filet mignon of cured meats. It was abundantly clear that everything on the table was of the highest quality.

After a few bites, Signore Gismondi raised his glass and turned to look at Adriana. It only took moments for his sons to follow suit. She realized that the first toast of the evening would be directed towards her, so she rested her fingers on the base of her glass.

"To new beginnings and the promises of a good future. *Salute!*"

The Gismondi sons echoed their father, each taking a long sip of wine.

Adriana modestly inclined her head towards Signore Gismondi. She had never had an easy time being the center of attention, and she felt slightly guilty that he would toast her in such a lovely manner when her only plan was to gather what she needed and disappear. Adriana reassured herself by chalking it up to a necessary evil.

She waited until Signore Gismondi took a second sip of his wine, before she took one herself, remembering to pace herself. Conversation and wine were two things that flowed freely and, if it was like anything she had heard about, it was going to be hours before the dinner was done.

While there were several carafes on the table, she glanced at one of the open and waiting bottles on the buffet and saw that the wine was a Lambrusco di Sorbara. The acidity of it rounded out the flavors of the meats and cheeses perfectly. Adriana was sorely tempted to forget what she had just resolved about the wine but she knew she needed a clear head, if for no other reason than to not slip up and give everything away. Besides, displays of drunkenness were looked down upon and she did not want to risk that.

Adriana looked over at Signore Gismondi and gave him a warm smile. "Everything is delicious, Signore."

Signore Gismondi briefly bowed his head. "This is just the beginning."

There were many conversations going on between the brothers and Signore Gismondi that it was impossible for Adriana to keep up with all of them, though she was quite proud of herself that even when they spoke their fastest, she had not even the slightest bit of trouble in understanding what they were saying. At no point, did she ever feel the least bit excluded.

They all effortlessly switched between talking with her and with each other.

At one point, Valentino caught Adriana's attention. "Have you found a favorite pizzeria yet?"

Adriana nodded. "I'm fortunate enough that it's right on the other side of the street from my gallery. I like my pizza with pancetta and I think they make it best of all the ones I've tried so far."

Sergio was the next to speak. "I've always thought the place over on the west side of town makes the best."

Before Adriana could reply, Ignacio shook his head at his little brother. "Sorry Sergio, but she's right."

Despite him being the most obstructed from her view, Adriana caught a flash of something in Sergio's eyes that she could not quite pinpoint. Worry lightly flickered in her chest as she was desperate to not irritate anyone. "I don't think I've gotten over to that pizzeria yet. Perhaps I'll have to give it a try soon."

Sergio's only response was a brief look, before he turned his gaze away, taking a long sip of his wine.

Valentino gave her a smile that conveyed that she should not worry about Sergio. "I know your favorite place. It's mine too. They also do great things with their prosciutto."

Adriana gave him an appreciative smile. "I completely agree."

She was not sure how much time had passed when they all were finished with their antipasto. It seemed to go quickly yet slowly in a relaxed way. Signore Gismondi rose and reached out for Adriana's plate.

She made to reach for it herself to hand to him but stopped, when he held up his hand towards her.

"That is not necessary. I've got it." He smiled down at her.

Adriana tried to return his smile as she settled her hands back on the table. The extent of his courtesy with her still had her boggled. If someone had told her a few years ago that an elusive criminal mastermind would be collecting her plate, glass and cutlery, she would have thought them insane.

"Sergio," Signore Gismondi waited until he had Sergio's full attention. "Help me carry these to the kitchen."

"Of course, Papà." Sergio's reply was automatic.

When the two left the room, Constantin caught Adriana's eye. "Do you paint your own paintings?"

"I'm afraid I don't." She lightly laughed. "Appreciating it, is as far as my artistic talent goes."

Constantin grinned in reply. "I never got past stick figures myself."

Dante broke off from his conversation with Macario. "Calling them stick figures is being quite generous!" His tone was entirely good-natured though.

Constantin laughed in at his brother's comment. "That's a fair enough point! Straight lines have never been my strong suit!"

Valentino grinned. "We keep telling you that's why rulers were invented!"

Sergio came into the dining room and took his seat. He had a quiet conversation with Ignacio, and Adriana thought she saw sullenness in his face, but she could not be sure.

Signore Gismondi entered a short while later, carrying a large tray with eight plates on it. Adriana thought it was a nice touch for him to bring the food out himself. He set her plate in front of her first, setting the others after that and saving his for last.

When she looked at her plate, Adriana tried to not choke. Sitting atop the risotto, was what she recognized as being white truffles. She had never even considered having an opportunity to taste them, and all the Gismondis were completely nonplussed by it. It was almost as if it was an everyday thing for them, and then she realized it probably was. Adriana wondered what it would have been like to grow up like that, to always have the best right at one's fingertips. She tried to ignore it, but she could not help the stab of envy she felt. She tried to remind herself that a good portion of that money had allegedly come from illegal activities.

With the first bite of the risotto, Adriana felt taste buds she had never known she had, start to awaken. The taste of the white truffles was indescribable and like nothing she had ever had before. She bit back a moan of pleasure and had to restrain herself to not start shoveling the dish into her mouth.

Adriana reached for her glass, curious to try the dish in combination with the next wine. Identifying wines had never been a particular strong suit of hers, so she was glad to sneak a glance at the bottle and see that it was a Barolo. She recalled that there was great strife between the traditionalists and modernists in regards to the wine production. Her hunch, based on everything she had been learning about Signore Gismondi, was that this wine fell into the traditionalist category. The taste of the wine danced in her mouth, as the intensity of it fell just shy of the intensity of the truffles, but the combination was a beautiful duet.

"Do you like to ski?" Dante asked her.

Adriana nodded. "I do. I've only been a couple of times, but I did enjoy it, even if the first time didn't go so well."

Ignacio laughed. "I'm certain it was much better than our first time!"

"What do you mean?" Her curiosity was piqued by the expression on everyone's face.

Valentino was as fast as lightning in his reply. "Hey, it's my turn to tell it this time!" He began the story. "The whole thing started when Papà had taken us on a trip to the Alps. Now, Macario, Dante and I had been several times before, so we were pretty good on skis at that point. Constantin, Ignacio and Sergio, not so much."

"Hey, the first couple of times down the slope went pretty good!" Constantin said in his defense.

"If only they could have kept going well," Ignacio spoke with amusement.

"Can I please continue the story?" Valentino waited until they both nodded. "So, Papà had been teaching them the basics, and it seemed like they had caught on."

"Sergio and I had at least!" Ignacio was quick on the defense. He responded to Valentino's look with a grin. "Sorry. Please, continue."

"To this day we still don't know how this was physically possible. So, Papà, Dante, Macario and I start heading down the slope, with Ignacio, Constantin and Sergio going at their own pace behind us. Well, at one point, Constantin loses control and slides into Ignacio but, rather than falling, the two keep going down the hill. Those two ended up running into Sergio and, somehow, they're all still upright and gaining more and more speed. None of us have any idea of what's happening. Macario was the next one they picked up along the way, then Dante. Out of us boys, I'm the fastest," he ignored the protests of the others and continued on as if they had not spoken, "so naturally I'm at the front. Next thing I know, my skis cross and I get sucked into the pack. We're all shouting at each other and trying to warn Papà, who can't hear us because of the wind. So, before he can realize what's happening, all of us are slamming into his back, and it was at this point that gravity finally takes over, and we all go plummeting to the ground. It was first a few meters before we all stopped rolling."

Along with the others at the table, Adriana laughed with abandon, the mirth bubbling up inside of her. She thought she saw Signore Gismondi close his eyes and smile, but she had no way of looking closer without being obvious. Even if she had seen correctly, she was certain his expression had to do with the memory itself, and nothing to do with her reaction. It was a short while before she could regain her breath. "What on earth did you all do after that?"

Signore Gismondi smiled warmly. "The only thing we could do. I picked the boys up, dusted them off, and we kept going until we reached the bottom."

Out of the corner of her eye, she caught Sergio smiling his first true smile of the evening. Adriana wondered briefly why he was so reserved compared to his brothers, and if he was always that way, or if it was just towards her.

When all were done with the primo, it was Constantin's turn to help Signore Gismondi with the dishes. Adriana felt slightly guilty for not helping out but it seemed the Gismondi patriarch would not hear of it, so she let it be what it was.

The intermezzo consisted of lemon sorbet and, while Adriana thought it exquisite, she was still a bit weirded out by having such a sweet dish between courses, rather than at the end.

This time Dante was the one who collected the dishes, along with his father.

Macario gave her a warm look. "Would you like to come outside with us?"

Adriana smiled in return. "Yes, that would be lovely."

Macario quickly stood up, pulling her chair out for her. Valentino and Ignacio rose as well and fell into step with the other two as they headed for the doors on the far side of the room.

When they stepped outside, Adriana had barely put her cigarette to her lips when Valentino held his already aflame lighter towards her. *"Grazie."* She was secretly relieved she did not have to dig around in her purse to find her own lighter. It always managed to slip into the most obscure place in the entire bag.

Darkness had set in as Adriana gazed up at the star filled sky. "It's amazing what a difference getting a bit out of the city can make. I don't remember the last time I saw so many stars. It's absolutely incredible."

Ignacio grinned. "When the summer nights were warm enough, all of us and Papà would grab our sleeping bags and spread them out on the grass and look up at them for hours until we all fell asleep. He taught us about all the constellations. To this day, we'll still come by with our kids and do the same."

"How many days until our camping trip?" Adriana's foster mother grinned down at her.

"The same as my age! 10!"

Adriana saw her fourteen-year-old foster "sister" roll her eyes and then shared a smirk with their other foster sister.

"So how many s'mores do you think you can eat?"

Adriana's eyes went wide. "We're going to get s'mores?!"

"As many as you want! Well, within reason," her foster mother followed up with a wink.

Eight days later, Adriana protested like she had never had before, when the social worker showed up and told her to pack her bags. She pleaded with her foster mother.

"There's nothing I can do. I wish that I could but I don't have control over this."

Adriana only stopped crying when she fell asleep in yet another strange bed.

For some reason, the thought of a man such as Signore Gismondi foregoing life's luxuries and sleeping on the grass was difficult for her to wrap her head around. For the second time that evening, Adriana had to subdue the stab of envy she felt. There were times in her life she would have given anything to have such memories.

Macario pointed up to the sky. "That's the north star there. Papà always told us that as long as we could find that, we could always find our way back home."

Despite home being something Adriana had always dreamt of having, it had always eluded her so she forced a smile, that did not quite reach her eyes. "That sounds very sweet."

When they sat back down at the table, it was Valentino who took the honors of helping her with her chair. She had to admit to herself that she was rather charmed by the chivalry. Of course, she was more than capable of doing things like opening a door or taking her seat unaided but, in a way, it made her feel respected, so she decided to enjoy it as long as she could.

Signore Gismondi and Dante returned, both bearing a tray for the secondo. Signore Gismondi laid the large plate and Dante placed the smaller one next to it, of course starting with Adriana.

The secondo consisted of a beef filet, grilled to a perfect medium, and drizzled with a dark sauce. On the second plate, which had been placed to the side of the larger plate, were squares of pumpkin, with the slightest hint of brown on the sides and sprinkled with rosemary and thyme.

With the first taste of the meat, Adriana identified the sauce as balsamic vinegar, and it gave the already perfect beef an extra flavor. She took a bite of the side dish and wondered why she had never considered roasting pumpkin before. The earthiness of the pumpkin, the acidity of the balsamic vinegar, and the savoriness of the beef combined to make a course that was nothing short of perfection.

This near holy trinity of food was perfectly rounded off by the Giramonte that accompanied the course.

Macario grimaced slightly as he watched his brother cutting up his beef filet. "Dante, for the thousandth time; it is not a patient!"

Adriana glanced between the two, a curious expression on her face.

Dante's expression was amused. "You'll have to forgive Macario," he said while looking at Adriana. "He has never been able to stand that my table manners are superior to his. He tries accounting it to my profession, never mind it has been that way since before I started my medical studies!" He finished with a laugh.

Despite the face Macario made at Dante, she could tell there was no real malice between the two. It seemed more like a cross between habit and tradition. Adriana could easily see it happening at every Gismondi family dinner.

Macario leaned towards her with a conspiratorial expression on his face. "Dante just likes to think that. I will always have more years of experience in certain things than he does, and it's a fact he would rather ignore!"

Adriana lightly laughed to mask the pain in her heart. Having a sibling rivalry that went on for decades had always been something she had longed for. Why some people had had the luck to be born into the right family is something she had always felt as grossly unfair.

The dinner was only at the halfway mark, when Signore Gismondi and Macario carried the plates to the kitchen.

Ignacio gave her a warm smile. "Here's a very deep and meaningful question for you-if you could only ever have one kind of biscotti ever again, which one would that be?"

It took only a second for Adriana to reply. "Hazelnut biscotti. Sometimes I have to remind myself that they're not a suitable breakfast!"

Constantin's face was full of sweet sadness. "I'm sure it is safe to say that we're all in agreement with you. And our mamma would remind us of the exact same thing!"

Macario came in at that moment and grinned. "Even on our birthdays we couldn't get her to relent!"

The love that the Gismondi sons still had for their mother was crystal clear and Adriana found herself wondering just what sort of woman could love a man such as Signore Gismondi and bear so many of his children.

The next platter that Signore Gismondi carried in, was covered with grapes and figs and asiago d'allevo and mascarpone cheese. Adriana was almost certain the mascarpone had a homemade look to it. It seemed all the stops were being pulled out for tonight's dinner. She was not sure what to make of that.

This time the wine was white and as it was being poured, she noted that it was a Cervaro Della Sala.

Adriana overheard a conversation between Constantin and Valentino which quickly caught her attention.

"Lorenzo's been pestering me for over a week to get him a pet snake but Paola has threatened me with divorce if that happens."

"Sorry but I have to agree with your wife on this!" She gave a little shudder. "To say I'm not fond of them would be putting it mildly. There is just something so wrong about anything that can move that fast without legs!"

"I'm sure Ignacio will agree wholeheartedly with you!" Macario said, while Constantin and Valentino grimaced ever so slightly.

Ignacio cringed at the memory. "You two," he said while pointing to Constantin and Valentino in turn, "had a large part to play in that!" At Adriana's confused expression, he continued. "Papà had taken all of us to the zoo. A few of us were looking at a king cobra. It was sitting up, or whatever it's called when the upper half of the snake is upright, and its' hood was out and I was absolutely entranced. Well those two noticed my distracted state and decided to grab me. Right at that precise moment, the snake jutted forward and hit the glass! I don't think I've ever screamed so loud in my life."

Constantin's expression was laced with regret. "We didn't know something like that was going to happen, but it really is no excuse. I'll just say, it was weeks before Giuseppe had to touch a dirty dish again."

"We deserved it though." Valentino admitted and Constantin nodded his agreement.

"Papà had to carry me around the zoo the rest of the day!" Ignacio's expression was tinged with embarrassment.

"And I would have done it every time after that, for as long as needed, if it had been necessary." He looked around the table. "You know that ensuring the safety and security of all of you is my greatest responsibility in life."

When the brothers broke off into conversation, Adriana looked at Signore Gismondi. Her voice was low as she tried to mask her emotion. She had never been the type to hold grudges, mostly because so many had been held against her, even for small things, that she was tired of them. Not all of her foster families had been like that, but it was a memory that still stuck out clearly and overshadowed the others. "It's incredible how you were able to forgive your sons so easily."

"There is not a single mistake that any of my children can make that I would not forgive."

Adriana had to admit to herself that she could not imagine a better father than Signore Gismondi. Almost everything she had seen and learned about him in the past couple of days seemed to be in complete juxtaposition to everything she thought she knew.

Macario gave her a warm smile. "Needless to say, the sand castle incident had a much happier outcome."

Dante grinned at the memory. "There was one time when we all were at the beach, and we each wanted to build a sand castle. Well, Papà gave us designated areas to avoid any squabbling. Of course, we go right up to the limits of our areas and before we knew it, we had a giant sand castle that stretched across the beach!"

Signore Gismondi smiled. "And what was the lesson you all learned from that?"

The Gismondi sons spoke in unison and without hesitation. "That things turn out best when we all work together and help each other out."

Signore Gismondi gave a satisfied nod, his face full of pride that the lesson was still remembered after so many years.

Adriana hid her sadness behind her smile. The way they all interacted with each other, it was clear they were a tight knit family. While some of her foster families had been kind, she and they had always known there was a limit on the time she would be with them, so the opportunity to really feel like a part of a family had always evaded her.

"You must be a very proud father, Signore Gismondi."

"I'm extremely proud of all of my children."

Adriana felt like icicles of fear had been placed in her blood, when she noted the intensity in his eyes. He was an extremely composed man, but she could tell that Signore Gismondi's passion, especially for his family, ran deep. She realized if she was caught, he would not just take it as an attack on himself, but on his sons as well. Adriana could not fail, if she hoped to get out of the situation alive.

This time Valentino accompanied his father with the dirty dishes.

Adriana was starting to feel that she could not possibly eat another bite, partly due to the amount of food she had consumed and partly due to the blazing nerves she was feeling, when Signore Gismondi walked in with the dessert. Eight small chocolate cakes adorned the tray and when her cake was placed in front of her, she was certain it had just come from the oven.

When she dug her spoon into it, a melted white fondant oozed out in the most appetizing fashion. If she had not been so distracted, she would have thought the taste heavenly, and would have claimed it to be the best dessert she had ever had. She could not even really note how the pairing with the sweet and elegant Il Recioto rounded off the last of the food for the evening perfectly.

When Ignacio helped his father, Adriana realized that the plate clearing was a perfect opportunity for Signore Gismondi to talk and solidify a plan with all of his sons. She felt the hairs on the back of her neck stand up and she fought to compose herself and keep an even face.

Adriana did not note so much of the espresso and finally the limoncello nor the conversations she partook in. It was all a blur as she battled with the building anxiety. Even when Macario had quietly asked her if everything was okay, she felt she was just barely able to convince him that all was fine.

She was almost too distracted to notice all the Gismondi men standing up, signaling the end to the dinner.

Adriana quickly stood up, not even noting Signore Gismondi pulling her chair out for her, and she was trying to figure out just how to convey an appropriate appreciation for the evening when Signore Gismondi interrupted her thoughts.

"Could you come with me to my office? There is a matter of great importance that I must discuss with you."

Adriana felt her heart triple in speed as her stomach twisted into knots. She felt she now knew with certainty that she had been wrong about the whole situation. He must have known exactly who she was and what she had been up to. Had the past couple of days just been an elaborate, twisted game? Had he just been fattening up the lamb before the slaughter? Had his sons been part of the deception? Perhaps that was the reason for Sergio's attitude towards her. Maybe he was the only one opposed to the idea but got dragged into it anyway. It took every ounce of self-control, but Adriana managed to keep her face even. "Of course, Signore."

He once more held out his arm to her, and Adriana did her best to hide her shaking as she weaved her arm around his. He led her out of the room.

The Revelation

Her palms sweated as she stood with Signore Gismondi in his office. Adriana wondered if she would die in this home. The Li Fonti painting hanging on the wall behind Signore Gismondi's desk did not even catch her attention, she was that distracted.

"Do you know one of the greatest pains a human being can face?"

The reports she had read of what he had done, arranged, or at the very least condoned, raced through her mind but she bit down on her tongue. She did not even want to imagine what he might have in store for her. "I do not, Signore."

Signore Gismondi looked directly into her eyes, his turbulent emotions nearly bubbling through. "The pain of having a child ripped from you, to have lead after lead after lead result in nothing, only to finally find her and not be able to pull her into your arms again."

Adriana's breath caught in her throat, as she finally noted the fervency of his eyes and face. Her heart tripled in speed, as she struggled to brace herself. She was so focused on being outed that his words were not really registering in her head. "What do you mean, Signore?"

Pain crossed Signore Gismondi's features. "I'm not Signore to you." His voice was soft, and every bit as powerful. "I'm your papà."

"What?!" That was all Adriana could manage to splutter out.

Signore Gismondi took a deep breath. "I love and cherish all my children. Very, very much. But every time your mother told me she was pregnant, I kept hoping for a little girl. My wish finally came true with you. We had a few precious months together, when you were taken from us."

Adriana's mouth opened and closed, trying to process everything that was being thrown at her.

"The story is long and very complicated… and I will share it all with you one day…" He looked over to his desk and picked up a silver picture frame. "If you have any doubts… look at this." He held the picture out to Adriana.

Despite her urges, Adriana looked at it. The picture showed a little infant with a pink, elastic band around her head. The birthmark on the side of her neck was displayed as one of pride.

Adriana's hand flew to that own spot on her neck. She felt that there was no way she could deny it. The mark was the one she had seen in the mirror for as long as she could remember. "This… this can't…" Her voice trailed off.

Signore Gismondi set the picture down, his eyes never leaving her. He reached out his hands, cradling her face, his thumbs tracing light circles over her cheekbones. *"Tesorino mio,"* he murmured, staring at her as if she were the most special being on the planet.

Adriana tried to form some words, but they all became choked in her throat.

"Tesorino mio," Signore Gismondi said, as a tear spilled over from his eye.

Adriana wanted to scream and pull away and run but she was fixed in place.

"Tesorino mio," Signore Gismondi whispered with reverence, moving his hands from her face to her back, drawing her in as close as possible, as he rested his head on top of hers. "You are never going to be without your papà again, *tesorino mio,* nor the rest of your family. Your brothers and I… we're never going to let you go again."

The panic finally bubbled up enough and Adriana found herself tearing away from Signore Gismondi. A mere second after, she was sprinting out of the office and down the hall. She could hear him shouting something but she could not make out what, nor did she care to.

She threw the front door open, and stumbled down the steps. Her legs were pumping furiously as she ran down the driveway. She had no idea where she was going to go; she just knew that she needed to get away.

She was about halfway to the gate, when Macario's car flew past her, then turned a sharp right, blocking Adriana's path. The second the car was parked he stepped out and swept around it, stopping directly in front of Adriana. "Please wait. We need to talk." His eyes were every bit as pleading as his voice.

Adriana came to a full stop just before him. Something finally clicked in her head. "You knew." Her voice was a mixture of astonishment and betrayal and wonder. "From the moment you stepped foot in my gallery, you knew."

Macario bowed his head briefly, before meeting Adriana's gaze. "Did I know 100%? No. Was I 99% sure? Yes." He hesitated briefly before he continued. "I'd like to think I'd know my baby sister anywhere. And it was like I was seeing Mamma, again." The tenderness in his voice was nearly heartbreaking.

This only caused Adriana to freak out more. "Was that the reason you even came by at all? To check me out? See if I was good enough?" She battled to hold her insecurities down, but she was losing.

Macario vehemently shook his head. "Not at all. The second Papà was told about you, he called us in to meet with him. He wanted to bring you out and tell you everything right away. I told him it was a terrible idea. How much pressure would that put on you?

"I convinced everyone that I was the best to reach out to you first. It took just about everything in my power, but Papà and our brothers finally agreed."

"What was the plan after that?" Adriana tried to spit the words out, but she was failing.

Macario met her gaze straight on. "To get you out here and get something to test your DNA against us and Papà. Though to be perfectly honest, Papà was ready to relent when we saw your birthmark and I nearly was too, but for all of our sakes, I knew we needed to have a concrete answer. I couldn't risk anybody getting a broken heart."

"How did you get a sample of my DNA?!"

"One of your cigarette butts and one of the glasses you drank from during lunch, to be sure."

"DNA tests take days, weeks to run! How could you possibly know the results already?"

"It helps that one of our brothers is the most respected surgeon in the area. He requested the tests be pushed to the front of the line. Just after midnight, we all knew the truth."

Adriana just barely bit back the urge to snap if he actually knew what the word "requested" meant for that was something she could not imagine any of them doing. "So, there's no doubt?" She had been hoping there might be a chance for that. But now that that was gone…

"None at all." He reached into the inner pocket of his blazer and pulled out several sheets of paper. "You can see for yourself, right here." He held the paper out towards her.

Adriana did not take it, but she did indeed look at it under the powerful light of the full moon. There were a lot of letters and numbers that she did not understand, but it was nicely summed up at the bottom of her and Signore Gismondi's results. *Probability of Paternity: 99.9998%.* She knew that was the closest to certainty that such a test could give. Adriana shuddered, feeling sick to her stomach. Macario mistook it for her being cold and he slipped off his blazer, wrapping it over her shoulders.

She took a couple of steps back, shivers still shooting up and down her spine. For nearly several decades, she had so many questions about her biological family. These were not the answers she had been hoping for. "Just what are you all expecting of me?"

"We aren't expecting anything. We're just hoping you'll give us a chance. That's why Papà waited until after dinner, to tell you the truth. We wanted you to get to know us, to see who we really are. Saying we knew the news would be a shock for you is a massive understatement, which is why we thought it was best to wait a few hours. I'm so, so sorry if that was the wrong decision." By the bright light of the moon, Adriana could make out a couple of tears glistening in Macario's eyes.

Adriana felt tears spring into her eyes as well, the difference being hers were angry. "None of you have any idea what it's been like for me! Bouncing around from home to home, year after year. Trying so hard to not get attached to anyone, because I might be gone the next day! To not even be happy on my birthday because I had no reason to celebrate it!"

"I know it's not the same, but we've had our pain too. We could never smile on your birthday, because we had no idea where you were, and the only thing we could hope for was that you were alive and okay. To have a cloud over every family celebration because we knew you should be there with us." His expression was contrite. He did not need to verbalize that what had transpired that night had been a collective dream for them for years.

Adriana felt as if someone had plunged a dagger in her heart, but she struggled not to let his words get to her. "Just what the hell am I supposed to do?"

"Just stay here, tonight. Please. We can figure everything else out tomorrow."

Adriana made up her mind. Just because they shared some DNA, it did not mean she had to be a part of that family. She would stay true to her mission.

Adriana would merely play her part, until she got what she needed and then, she would never have to see them again.

"All right. I'll stay tonight."

Macario's eyes were a mixture of complete joy and complete desperation. "Would you let your *fratellone* give you a hug?"

Big brother. She had had a few of those over the years but none of them had lasted. He would be no different. Adriana hesitated, and then slightly nodded. She was surprised by the speed Macario's arms wrapped around her.

"*Bentornato a casa, sorellina.*" His voice was as soft as a breeze, but just as powerful.

Welcome home, little sister. If that made them bring her into the fold, so to say, that much quicker, then that was a sentiment she could live with for a short while.

He quickly kissed the top of her head, letting her go enough to lead her over to the car.

While Macario walked back around to the driver's side, Adriana took a deep breath. She was going to be nothing more than a character in a play, and she would not let them get to her.

The Reunion

Adriana remembered Macario's propensity for being a gentleman as he parked in front of the house, and waited until he opened the door for her. He kept a hand on her back as they walked up to the front door.

It was just wide enough for them to go through, when she saw Signore Gismondi rushing towards them. "*Grazie a Dio!*" The second he could, he pulled her into his arms again. "Please, don't scare your Papà like that again, *tesorino mio*."

Adriana fought to not be utterly tense. "I'm sorry." She gave him a little squeeze and tried to not sigh with relief when he finally let go of her.

Her reprieve was only momentary though, as he took her by the hand and led them to the sitting room where the others were waiting. He was bursting with joy when he regarded them. "My boys, you can finally and truly welcome your sister home."

Valentino was the first one forward. "*Bentornato a casa.*" His eyes were shining with happiness, as he kissed Adriana's cheek, before wrapping his arms around her.

Ignacio came next, followed by Dante, then Constantin. There was a look that passed between Sergio and Signore Gismondi that Adriana did not understand, before he did as his brothers had done. His hug was neither as long nor as tight as the others had been.

"All my children in the same room. This has been a better evening than anything I could have ever imagined!"

Macario smiled warmly. "You can appreciate it more tomorrow, Papà. Right now, I think we could all do with some rest. Our sorellina's agreed to stay here tonight."

"Are you tired?" Signore Gismondi questioned her.

Adriana nodded her head. "A bit yes. It's been a lot to process…"

"Then we will get you some rest. Come, I'll show you your room." He held his arm out to her.

There was a chorus of good nights, which Adriana returned before Signore Gismondi led her to the stairs. The hallways seemed to stretch on for an eternity. They finally came to a stop before a room, which was right next to a set of double doors at the end of the hall. Adriana guessed those doors led to Signore Gismondi's room.

He opened the door and led her in. The room was gigantic and Adriana was pretty sure it was the size of her entire flat in the States. There was a huge bed in the middle, and dark wood furniture was placed throughout. To the left there were two doors, one which stood ajar. She could make out a bathroom and surmised that the other must be for a closet.

"Whatever you don't like, we will change immediately."

Adriana put on a soft smile. "It's beautiful." At least that was something she did not have to lie about.

Signore Gismondi beamed. "I hope you don't mind but I took the liberty of getting you some things."

"You didn't have to do that."

"I couldn't help myself." He pointed to a large dresser over to the right. "There are some pajamas and some clothes there, as well as in the closet. Just say if there's anything you need. I won't have my princess go without."

Adriana nodded, trying to look grateful. "Thank you."

Signore Gismondi cradled her face once more. "*Buona notte. Sogni d'oro, tesorino mio.*" He tilted her head down and pressed his lips to her forehead.

"*Buona notte.*" Adriana waited until he softly shut the door behind him, before she sharply exhaled. She went over to the dresser and grabbed the first pair of pajamas she could find, not even taking note of the more than a few things. Adriana hurried for the bathroom and threw the faucet on with haste.

The first sob was soft, barely even audible to her. The next one was stronger, as was everyone after that until she was crumpled on the floor, gasping for air as the tears raced down her cheeks. She beat her hand on the soft bath mat, wanting to tear it to shreds.

She had no idea if it had been minutes or hours, but the tears finally abated. It took all of her willpower to pull herself up off the floor. Even in her distraught state, the prospect of sleeping on cold tiles held no appeal. Adriana slipped out of her clothes as quickly as she could and put on the pajamas. She stumbled over her own feet as she made way for the bed, just barely able to throw the covers back before she crawled in. It was only seconds after her head hit one of the many pillows that she was asleep.

The Story

Adriana started when she awoke, confused to where she was, before the memories from the night before came flooding back to her. She took a couple of deep, steadying breaths before climbing out from the bed. She took a glance at her clothes, which were a crumpled heap on the bathroom floor. Shaking her head, she figured she could amuse Signore Gismondi and wear whatever it was he had bought for her. Adriana walked over to the closet and gasped when she opened the door.

Her mouth hung open as she saw the contents of the large, walk-in closet. There were dozens of dresses and pants and tops, ranging from silk to cashmere to merino wool. There was even a whole section of long, soft sweaters. Everything was top of the line and in pristine condition. If Adriana had the timeline of events right, he had gone out and bought her almost an entire wardrobe in a matter of hours. She was certain he did not give a second thought to using more money at one time than most people would ever see in a decade.

Overwhelmed by the options, she grabbed a long-sleeved dress, cut in the latest style, a charcoal grey cardigan, and found a pair of shoes that would go with it. One glance earlier had told her, that her pair had not survived her sprint down the driveway all that well.

Adriana was a bit unsettled that everything seemed to fit. Had Signore Gismondi hired somebody to break into her flat and rummage through her things? Had he paid off the super to let the person in? How else could he have found out her sizes? Had that been the real reason he had Macario bring her out the other day? So, Signore Gismondi could have somebody invade her personal space and dig around to see if there was anything to find?

When she was dressed, she went into the bathroom and found a silver hairbrush sitting on the counter. She did what she could with her hair, after digging out a clip from her purse and pinning up the sides, similar to how it had been the night before. It hid the worst of it.

Adriana stared at her reflection for several long moments, while she breathed deeply. "You can do this." She whispered. "The more you play your part, the quicker they will be to let you in and you can get what you need and be gone." One more breath, and Adriana headed out of the room.

As she made her way down the stairs, the smell of fresh baked cornetti greeted her. She followed the scent and found the kitchen. If nothing else, she could ask Giuseppe where the Gismondis were. She pushed on the swinging door.

Adriana was shocked to find Signore Gismondi pulling the baking tray out of the oven. She thought for sure he would never bother with something like that himself.

A wide smile broke on his face when he saw her. Signore Gismondi hurriedly set the tray down and strode over to her. "*Buongiorno, tesorino mio!*" He placed his hands on her arms as he kissed both her cheeks. "Did you sleep well?"

Adriana nodded. "Probably the best night's sleep I've had in a while."

"Of course! It's because you're finally home." He smiled at her as he headed over and started removing the cornetti from the tray. "I'm glad you found something that you liked," he indicated her dress with a wave.

"It's all wonderful…. but it's too much. I can't accept all of that!" She had decided that it was best to show a little resistance, rather than falling into the role so quickly.

He waved his hand dismissively. "You can and you will. Nothing but the best, for my princess. Besides, that's nothing compared to what I have planned for your birthday."

Adriana seriously hoped she would be gone long before then. She plastered on a smile instead.

He picked up the plate and guided Adriana out of the kitchen. "Come. Your brothers are waiting."

She tried to remember the way as they walked. The sooner she learned the house, the easier time she would have sneaking around.

Signore Gismondi's sons were talking boisterously when they entered. All attention turned towards Adriana.

This time, Ignacio was the first to greet her. "Good morning, sleepy head." He teased her with affection.

Dante rolled his eyes. "You are genuinely not one to tease someone about that, Ignacio!"

There was a round of kisses before they all settled down at the table, Adriana once again seated on Signore Gismondi' s right.

"Two meals, in a row, made by you, on a weekday, Papà? Giuseppe must be worried that you're going to fire him!" Macario teased his father.

Adriana looked over at Signore Gismondi in surprise. "The dinner last night? You made that?"

Signore Gismondi set his cappuccino down and squeezed her hand. "You don't think that I'd let my daughter's first family dinner back home be made by someone else, do you?"

She looked down at her plate. She had not given it much thought. As much as she tried not to, she felt touched by what he had said and she hated herself for it.

"Your brothers have said they'd be happy to go by your place, get your things, and bring them back here."

"Bring them here?" Adriana could not hide her confusion.

"Papà," Valentino intervened. "We said we'd be happy to do that, if that's what she wants."

"Of course, she wants to move back home! Don't you, my princess?" Signore Gismondi held her gaze.

"I...I haven't really thought about it."

Macario looked between her and Signore Gismondi. His gaze rested on his father. "Remember how we talked about not pressuring her, Papà."

Signore Gismondi scoffed. "What pressure are you talking about? Her rightful place is here."

Adriana could feel the tension rising in the room and did not want it erupting. She spoke quickly. "I suppose it could be nice... but my gallery."

"I've already spoken with Ignacio's wife, Bellissa. She's an antiques expert but has a side passion for paintings. She has told me she'd be happy to cover for you for as long as needed. It'll give you time to settle in and I'll have found a driver for you by then." The sharp nod he gave signaled the matter had been settled.

Macario gave her a sympathetic look. She tried to smile in return.

"I apologize in advance for the mess. I don't think anything is growing on the dishes... yet."

Constantin slammed his hand on the table. "All these years, I tried telling Paola that it was genetic and she never believed me!" He pointed at Adriana. "You must tell her that when you meet."

Adriana arched an eyebrow. "You want me, to tell your wife, that hating doing dishes, is a genetic predisposition?" She considered it for a few moments. "All right."

There were laughs all around the table. Dante took a quick sip of his cappuccino before he spoke. "You two, Ignacio and Sergio... like peas in a pod."

While Ignacio grinned, Sergio looked over to the side. Adriana got the feeling he held a certain negativity towards her but she could not figure out what. She noted to be extra cautious around him.

Breakfast was finished a short time later and Signore Gismondi's sons bid them goodbye. Adriana had turned her keys over to Ignacio, along with the code for the alarm system at the gallery. As much as she hated it, she knew guarding that code while she was supposedly happy to be a part of the family would not make much sense.

When they were all gone, Signore Gismondi wrapped an arm over her shoulders. "Come with me.

There's something I want to show you." He led the way through the house and to the library.

Sun was pouring in the floor-to-ceiling glass at the end of the room, a light breeze making the trees sway as if in a dance. She still thought it an incredible sight.

They stopped in front of the desk, where an ornate silver box was sitting. It was intricately carved, with more tiny details than could be estimated at a glance. Adriana was pretty sure it could cover at least several months of rent for her.

Signore Gismondi picked up the box. "This was the first gift I ever gave you." He held it out to her.

Adriana took it, and nervously opened it. The interior was deep red velvet, and there was something engraved in the middle of the lid. A soft tone filled the room, and she only heard a few notes when she gasped in surprise. "Scarlatti's Keyboard Sonata in E minor. It's… it's always been one of my favorites!"

Signore Gismondi smiled broadly. "I would let it play every night, while I would rock you to sleep."

"You… you did that?" She questioned with wonder, while the music box played away.

"It was my most favorite part of the day." The smile that crossed his face was sentimental. "The box belonged to my mother. You are named after her."

She looked closely at the engraving. "Lucia…" Her voice was mere a whisper.

"Yes. I realize it will take you some time, but I'm looking very much forward to the day I get to call you Lucia again."

Tears welled in her eyes and the child part of her she had been trying to oppress this whole time rushed forward. For so many years she had wondered about where she came from, who her parents were, if she had a different name. Seeing just how much she was cared about got to her on a different level. One tear glided down her face, followed quickly by another. The only part she was playing right now was herself.

Signore Gismondi gently took the music box from her and set it back on the desk, the music still playing away. His arms enveloped her, one hand holding the back of her head, the other rubbing up and down her back. "Shhhh… *tesorino mio*. It's alright. Everything's going to be alright. Papà is right here."

Despite herself, she leaned against him, her arms curling up to his shoulders. She found herself wondering if that was how he held the infant her, when he would be rocking her to sleep.

Signore Gismondi continued stroking her back. As long as the tears kept coming, he kept holding her.

Adriana was hating the position she was being put in, and the conflict that was raging inside of her. "It's not fair!" The whisper was harsh and escaped her lips before she could think twice about it.

"I know it's not, *tesorino mio*. But I'm going to do whatever it takes. I promise you that."

Adriana finally felt the tears abating and she pulled back, looking up at Signore Gismondi.

He cupped her face. "It breaks my heart to see you like this. Tell me what I have to do to make it better."

Not be you, she thought. As a father, he was everything she had ever dreamed of. As a person, not so much. Adriana knew for her own sake that she should not ask what she was about to but she could not help herself. "Tell me about my mother." Details of Signore Gismondi's wife had been sparse and Adriana had not paid much attention to what little information there was. At that point, it was a huge regret for her.

"Her name was Rosalia." He pulled his wallet out of his pocket and took a picture out. "This is what she looked like."

Adriana's smile was soft as she stared at the picture. A woman with short, dark hair and sparkling eyes grinned up at her. If it was not for the different hairstyle and the clothes that gave the decade away with a mere glance, she would have felt like she was looking in the mirror, rather than at a photograph. None of the files had ever had a picture of her, but Adriana was not sure she would have even considered the possibility of being Rosalia's daughter if she had seen such a picture. Awareness did often lead to greater observations, as the old sentiment went. "What happened to her?"

Signore Gismondi got a faraway look in his eyes. "Shortly after you were born, she fell ill. The illness spread quickly and after three months, there was nothing that could be done." He paused, taking a deep breath. "Two weeks after the funeral, you were taken."

Her eyes widened with shock. "You... you lost your wife... and me... in the span of less than a month?"

He swallowed hard. "There has never been a darker period in my life."

Before she could think about what she was doing, she reached out and wrapped her arms around Agostino. Surely something like that could drive people to do things they normally would not. What if grief or desperation had driven him down a dark path he would not have otherwise followed?

A heartbeat later, Agostino folded his arms around her. "I missed you so much, *tesorino mio*. I don't know what I'd do if anything ever happened to you again."

She decided to think about the consequences later. "I'm here now."

"Yes, you are," Agostino said with a smile on his face. "Come, let us take a walk in the garden."

She nodded her consent, leaning on him as they walked out the door.

The Confrontation

Adriana and Agostino walked around the house when they heard the commotion that could only signal the return of his sons. She was slightly surprised by what quick work they had made of her apartment.

Macario looked over, a box under one arm and a suitcase in the hand. "Sorellina, I will have you know I had to call Ciana to make sense of more than half of the stuff in your bathroom. How many different face washes do you really need?"

She smirked at him. "It all depends on the situation."

"Funny, those were her exact words as well." He grinned at her. "Though apparently, she was appalled when she heard the brand. She told me to chuck them in the bin and met me in town and gave me proper stuff to give to you."

While Adriana was a little offended, she was also touched. "You'll have to pass on my thanks to her."

Macario nodded as he followed after his brothers. "The sorting is all on you though!" He had such an easy time with the suitcase that Adriana would have thought there was nothing in it, if she did not know better.

"I have to correct your brother on that." Agostino said as they headed into the house. "You just have to decide how you would like it, and Marie will take care of the rest when she returns tomorrow."

Just one more trip was needed before they were all in the sitting room again. "Thank you all for your help."

"It was nothing, sorellina!" Valentino said with a grin.

"I'm done! I'm out of here!" Sergio suddenly shouted. He started storming for the door.

Agostino's voice cracked like a whip. "Sergio, you stop it this instant!"

"Sergio, what have I done wrong?" Adriana called after him.

The ferocity with which he turned made Adriana take a couple of steps back.

"What haven't you done wrong??"

"Stop it, Sergio," Ignacio hissed at his little brother.

Sergio took a couple of steps towards her, the aggression almost tangible. "Everything just always had to be about you! Every single little thing, it was always Lucia this and Lucia that! I haven't been able to have a single moment that wasn't spoiled by you!"

"I didn't ask for that!"

"And I didn't ask to lose my mother! And I wouldn't have, if it wasn't for you!"

Adriana felt like she had been punched in the gut. Fear took over a moment later.

While all of the brothers made to move to Sergio, Macario was the first to reach him. He was practically nose to nose with Sergio. The older brother's face was set in a snarl. "Don't you blame that on her! Don't you dare!"

"Sergio," Agostino growled. "You apologize to your sister! Immediately!"

Sergio met his father's eyes. "You know, Papà, you've always told us we all have our roles in the family. What's hers going to be? Hmmm? The family whore?"

Adriana shouted as Macario's hands grabbed onto the front of Sergio's shirt. Sergio started trying to push him off.

"Stop it!" she screamed. She ran towards the two, slipping past Constantin, who tried to stop her. She grabbed onto Macario's arm, trying to pull him off. "Stop it!"

The next thing she knew, Sergio's elbow slammed into her cheek, and the force from it caused her to lose her balance and fall to the hardwood floor, landing on her back. She rolled over and tried to push herself up.

Despite the pain and the tears springing in her eyes, she was well aware of just how eerily still the room had gotten.

"Dante," Agostino said, his voice barely containing his rage.

Dante did not need to be told what was expected of him. He immediately reached down and helped her up, one arm around her waist and the other on her arm. "I've got you," he whispered.

"Take your sister to the kitchen and get her some ice. Now."

Adriana looked over at Agostino and shrank down against Dante. The storm that was in Agostino's eyes was nothing short of terrifying. She managed to dredge up some courage, knowing none of that was directed at her. "It was an accident!"

Agostino would not look at her. His eyes were fixed on Sergio. "Dante."

Dante nodded and gently pulled her towards the door. "Just come." His voice was as soft as he could make it, his arms still wrapped around her.

They were walking down the hallway, when she finally dared to speak again. "What's he going to do?"

"Nothing like what happened to your face, if that's what you're worried about." He gave her a soft look. "There are very few things in this world that can set

Papà off like that. He shouts, and he screams, and he'll throw things, but he'd never hit one of us. He just doesn't want you to see that side of him."

"It was horrifying…" Adriana was just grateful she had been spared the full explosion. The precursor had been more than enough for her.

Dante merely nodded. When they got to the kitchen, he sat her down on a stool by the marble island before going over to the freezer. He talked as he filled a bag with ice. "Don't misunderstand what I'm about to say. I'm not trying to defend what Sergio did and said by any means."

Adriana nodded, waiting for him to continue.

He grabbed a towel on the way and wrapped it around the bag. He sat in front of Adriana and placed the bag on her cheek as gently as he could. "Sergio, he was only one and a half years old when you were taken. He was too young to understand what was happening. He didn't have any memory of you." His smile was sad with tinges of bitterness. "Sometimes, we envied him for that."

Adriana squeezed his free hand. "It must have been so hard on all of you."

Dante nodded. "We helped each other through it, as much as we could. But there are some things that you just can't get over."

104

What Adriana thought was impossible happened. She was sure between last night and that morning she had cried herself dry, but now even more tears were welling up in her eyes. How could she have thought she could be so casual about everything, to just waltz in and out of their lives again?

"Hey, hey, sorellina. It's okay." Dante brushed the back of his fingers up and down her good cheek. "Let's take a look and see how it's doing, shall we?"

Adriana blinked rapidly, trying to get the tears out of her eyes. She nodded briefly.

He lifted the bag and surveyed the bruise, placing the ice on again. "Still needs a little more time but it should be okay."

Adriana tried to crack a smile. "Eh, I've survived worse." The moment the words were out of her mouth, she wished she could take them back. She avoided looking at Dante.

"What do you mean by that, sorellina?"

"Nothing," she tried to say evenly, still avoiding his gaze.

"What do you think you're doing?!?!"

Adriana's eleven-year-old self slunk down in the chair as she stared up at her enraged foster father. Her foster mother was hurriedly wiping up the spilled soda. "It...it was...an accident..."

"You think you can just waste my hard-earned money?!"

"I didn't mean to!"

Her breath caught in her throat as she felt the chair being yanked back. The next thing she knew, her foster father's hand was hurtling towards her…

Dante took her chin between his forefinger and thumb and slowly turned her head so she had to look at him. "Sorellina, I'm going to ask you again. What did you mean by you've survived worse?"

"I told you-nothing!" While Adriana had gotten very good at lying, there was something about the look in his eyes that was making it extremely hard for her to be dishonest with him.

"We can do this the easy way or the hard way. The easy way is you tell me what you're talking about. The hard way is I use a lot of time and resources to find out on my own."

She sighed, realizing there was no way out. After seeing the way Agostino had reacted when his own son accidently hit her, she could only imagine how he would react to what she was about to say. She was not sure she wanted to know. "First, you have to promise me that you won't tell anyone. And I mean anyone!"

His eyes flicked momentarily to something past her before returning. He nodded his consent.

"When I was a kid, I was in a lot of different foster homes. There was one in particular, that was clearly in it for the check. The foster dad... he smacked me around a few times."

Dante's face was much too even for Adriana to be comfortable. It was like the calm before the storm. She rushed on with her story.

"It was only a couple of times it happened. The last time, he forgot the social worker was visiting the next day. I was taken out of the home and he was sent to jail."

"Is he still there?"

"I don't know." Adriana said with complete honesty. "He would have been released for what he did to me but those types often end up back in prison. All I know is he was caught, he served his time and it's over."

"What was his name?"

"Dante." Adriana's voice was laced with nervousness. "I said it was over."

"As you wish," he said with a smile. Adriana was far from convinced.

"Just remember what you promised me."

He nodded, lifting the bag once more. "That should keep it down for now. We might need to do the whole thing again in a couple of hours, but I think it'll be okay."

"Thank you." Her voice made it clear she was not just referring to the ice.

As Dante was putting the bag back in the freezer, Agostino barreled into the kitchen. Macario was right behind.

"*Tesorino mio,*" Agostino made a beeline for her. "Are you okay?" He tilted her head so he could get a better look at the light bruise that was forming, despite Dante's best efforts. The pain in his eyes almost looked worse than Adriana felt.

"I'll be fine," she tried to reassure him. "Dante's been taking very good care of me."

"Sorellina, I am so, so sorry." Macario was almost pleading.

She looked over to him. "It's not your fault. The whole thing was an accident."

"No, the moment I felt your hands on my arm I should have let go."

"Macario, there was what, one or two seconds? Even if you had, there's no guarantee that what happened, wouldn't have happened. I'm going to be fine, okay?"

He nodded with great reluctance, his head hanging with shame.

She looked over at Agostino. "Where's Sergio?"

Agostino reached out and gently stroked her hair. "He's gone home but I promise you, he will never, ever do or say anything like he did today, ever again."

At first, she thought she was dying to ask what had happened in the sitting room. Then, she realized she actually did not want to know, even if she could get more than a vague answer.

She knew if they were to move on from this situation, she would have to initiate it. "Any chance I could get a glass of red wine?"

"Of course, my princess!" Agostino motioned for Dante to get the glasses while he hurried over to the wine cellar. He was back as quickly as possible, several bottles of wine in hand. Agostino filled her glass first and handed it to her before filling the others.

She took a sip. "Is this the same wine you served last night, with the *secondo*?"

Agostino nodded. "Yes, it is."

She smiled. "It was the best beef fillet, I've ever had."

The smile that graced his face was endearing. "It will be the first of many, my princess."

"It was probably best that you served it directly, otherwise I don't think Constantin would have let me have any."

"I heard that!" He said as he entered the kitchen with Ignacio and Valentino. "And you're absolutely right."

She was relieved when the others chuckled. The thought did cross her mind that she would have envied Constantin's metabolism, if not for the fact that hers was the same.

"But that could be true of just about any dish!" Valentino said, helping himself to the wine.

"We all have our weaknesses." She said with a shrug. "I make no promises when it comes to chocolate cake."

"I'll remember to guard mine, when I sit next to you!" Ignacio declared.

"Like you'd be able to say no, Ignacio!" Macario had finally lifted his head up.

"I could try!"

She smiled softly, relieved they were moving on. The brothers easily slipped into conversation. She was not consciously aware that there was yet another chink to her resolve with regards to her mission. Macario's protectiveness, Dante's tenderness, Ignacio's teasing, Constantin's joking, Valentino's happy help and even

110

Sergio's jealousy-it was the most real family experience she had ever had. She did not want to think about having to give it up, so she did not.

She felt Agostino's hand on her shoulder and she looked up at him.

He spoke softly. "I'm never going to let anything like that happen again. I swear it."

"You didn't let it happen this time either." She placed her free hand over his. She was well aware why he was so haunted over the whole thing. Mere hours after he told her he would pretty much lose his mind if anything were to happen to her; she ended up getting knocked to the floor. "Please, stop feeling so bad about this."

"For you, I will try." He pressed his lips to the top of her head.

She squeezed his hand while she watched her brothers.

The Memories

Adriana swung her feet out of the bed and stretched. It was, by far, the nicest bed she had ever slept in.

She ambled over to the closet and surveyed the contents. A couple of suitcases, which contained her old clothes, stood by the closet door, Marie first due to arrive back that day. Adriana's eyes went between the two sets and could not help but think that her own clothes were rather drab in comparison. She told herself she did have to dress the part, as she put together an outfit from the new clothes. After all, she was still on a mission, was she not?

When Adriana had finished her morning prep, she made her way downstairs. Agostino had told her breakfast would be waiting in the dining room, when she was ready for it.

Agostino was reading the newspaper, when she walked into the room. She was slightly surprised that he seemed to be waiting on her, given that it was later in the morning.

He looked up and quickly folded the paper, setting it to the side. *"Ciao, tesorino mio."*

"Ciao." She replied, putting on a smile. She had the feeling something was expected of her so when she reached Agostino, she bent down and gave him a peck on the cheek. This time she was across from him, at

least as far as she could gather due to the empty, waiting plate. "I'm sorry if I've kept you waiting for long."

"Not at all, *tesorino mio*. Breakfast is when you want it. My day is planned around you."

How he could make her feel so important, with a couple of sentences, she did not know but Adriana tried to not let it get to her too much.

Agostino pointed out the different trays sitting on the table. "The ones on the blue liner are regular cornetti, the ones on the green are with cream and the ones on the white are with jam."

Adriana took a jam filled cornetto and put it on her plate.

A soft smile graced Agostino's face. "That was your mother's favorite kind. She would say her morning hadn't really begun until she had one."

The mere mention of her mother commanded her full attention. "What else did she like?" She found herself desperate to know every little thing about the woman who had been denied to her.

Agostino's expression was one of reminiscing. "She loved to sing. Everything from lullabies to arias."

"I wish I could have heard her."

"That is still possible. Sergio took all of her old tapes and converted them to digital format. There are dozens of them on my computer.. I can play them for you sometime."

She broke out in a grateful smile. "I would love that."

"In the meantime, I have something else for you." He stood up and walked over to the buffet that stood by the wall. He took out a small key and unlocked the top drawer and took something out. He locked the drawer again before coming back and taking his seat once more. He held out the object to her.

When Adriana looked, she saw a platinum ring, covered in brilliant diamonds. Adriana carefully took it and turned her gaze to Agostino. "What is this?"

"It was your mother's wedding ring. She wanted you to have it."

Her eyes became moist as she stared at the ring. Adriana tried to tell herself she could not accept it, that she had no right to it, but the idea of having something of her mother's, was too much for her to turn away. Adriana knew she would have to leave it behind, when she left. She decided, though, that there was no reason to rush things. If there was anything to be found, it would still be there for a while. Besides, she did not want to raise suspicions so better to take the time that was needed.

As she looked closer at the ring, she noticed an engraving. "More love every day," she whispered.

"That was how we chose to live our life together."

She nodded, dabbing the corner of her eyes, before slipping the ring onto the ring finger on her right hand. It was a bit snug, but otherwise it was a perfect fit. It felt like having part of her mother with her.

"She would have been so proud of you."

Wonder filled her eyes as she looked at Agostino. "You loved her so much, didn't you?"

"Love." Agostino gently corrected. "She might be gone, but my feelings for her have never faded."

"I never thought love like that actually existed."

"It took something special, to create all of you." His eyes brimmed with emotion as he held her gaze for several long seconds. He gave her a meaningful smile before he continued. "I want to know everything about you. Everything you love, everything you hate."

"I don't really know where to begin."

"What foods don't you like? The sooner Giuseppe knows, the sooner he can alter the menu if need be."

Adriana hesitated. Being asked what foods she did and did not like was a new experience for her. She had never had the opportunity to be picky so she had learned to eat foods she did not really care for. Even when she was on her own, her budget, or lack thereof rather, determined a lot of her eating decisions. Adriana considered saying it was something Agostino should not concern himself with, but she had a feeling that would not be an adequate enough answer for him. "I don't really like seafood."

A sentimental smile graced Agostino's face. "Given how your mother was when she was pregnant with you, that doesn't surprise me at all."

"What do you mean?"

"While her loves and loathing were different with each of you, there was one thing that was common when she was pregnant with your brothers. She couldn't tolerate the smell of raw meat, nor of it being cooked. Sometimes, being on the other side of the house wasn't enough for her. She'd have to go for a walk around the garden. But with you, she couldn't stand the sight, or smell, or taste of anything that came from water. That was when I started getting my hopes up, that you were a girl."

"So, what was each love and loathing?"

There was no hesitation in his response. "With Macario, she couldn't eat enough Cerignola olives, but cherries had to be kept far away from her. With Valentino, she ate culatello on an almost daily basis, but sugar beets never came anywhere near her. With Dante, she'd eat lemons like they were oranges but she couldn't get within sniffing distance of a raw onion. With Constantin, she was constantly making Foccacia al Pomadoro but she never made a batch of amaretti, or anything else to do with almonds, for that matter. With Ignacio, she'd sprinkle balsamic vinegar on just about everything but avoided pears at all costs. With Sergio, mussels were her favorite but she nearly banned fennel from the house. With you, strawberries were the greatest food on the planet but she detested aubergine."

A soft smile graced her face. "I've never cared much for aubergine myself."

"She often wondered if that would be the case with you." There was a special sort of tenderness in his voice. "We can inform Giuseppe that seafood and aubergine are to be taken off the menu, when we're done with breakfast."

Adriana was somewhat surprised by his decisiveness. "If you like those things, I can handle eating them."

Agostino gave a wave of his hand. "I will not have you subjected to things you do not care for. Nothing more needs to be said on the matter."

She was quickly picking up on the special tone that Agostino had, when he felt a matter had been settled. Adriana did not want to push things and risk slipping out of his good graces, even ever so slightly, so she merely gave him a soft smile.

"I have one more thing for you." Agostino pulled his wallet out and took out a credit card, holding it out for her. "This is for whatever you may need or want."

When Adriana took the card, he continued. "That card is tied to my account. The pin number is 4038. Use it to your heart's desire. I expect to see several charges a week, at the very least."

"I'll do my best."

"What would you like to do today? I'm all yours."

She gave him a surprised look. "You don't have a lot of work to do?" For a reason unknown to her, Adriana had figured he would not want to take any more time away from his business than necessary.

"For the first, I have a very competent staff that is more than capable of running things while I am absent. For the second, and the most important, we've lost nearly thirty years together. I'm not going to let a single second go to waste."

Her breath caught in her throat as she looked at Agostino. There was no doubting the sincerity of what he said. She was at a complete loss for what to say but was saved when Marie entered the room.

Marie placed a cappuccino by her plate and gave her a warm smile. "I'm sorry if you've been waiting long for your coffee, Signorina Gismondi."

Her eyes widened, completely thrown by what the maid had just called her. Adriana had not even thought about how Giuseppe and Marie would address her. She tried to recover as quickly as possible, knowing that any objection to being called that would be a major red flag. "There's nothing to apologize for. I didn't even know when I would be getting up today!" She tried to give a reassuring smile.

"Would you like more breakfast?" Agostino questioned her.

"I suppose I could have one more," she said with a slightly guilty smile.

Agostino nodded, then looked at Marie. "When my daughter has taken her last piece, could you please take the rest of the cornetti to the kitchen again?"

"Of course, Signore!"

Adriana hastily grabbed a cream cornetto and tried to distract herself with that while Marie cleared the table.

When it was just her and Agostino again, she gave him a soft smile. "These are almost as good as the ones from yesterday."

"*Grazie, tesorino mio.* Your mother taught me everything I know about making them."

There was no doubt to her that Agostino had worshipped Rosalia and for a reason that she could not quite explain, she was positive that it was her mother who had always had the final word in the house, and not Agostino.

When breakfast was finished, she and Agostino made way for the kitchen. Adriana stopped in her tracks when she noticed a framed photograph out of the corner of her eye.

Sitting on a small table in the hallway, was a picture of an approximately forty years younger Agostino staring at his new bride, who was looking at him with equal adoration. In that moment, it seemed that no one else existed in the world but the two of them.

Hearing about what a happy relationship they had was one thing. Seeing it with her own eyes was completely another. She was breathless with emotion. The sound of Agostino's voice brought her back to the present moment.

"So many years ago, but it still feels like yesterday." Agostino's face was a mixture of emotions.

Sergio's words from the day before echoed in her mind and Adriana felt an illogical sense of guilt. Her birth was connected to her mother's death, no matter what they all said. Her voice was quiet when she spoke. "I'm so sorry you lost her."

"*We* lost her, *tesorino mio*." Agostino gently corrected her. "She lives on though, in each and every one of you."

She mustered as much of a smile as she could.

Agostino did not say anything, but instead, he wrapped his arm over her shoulders and gave it a soft squeeze. He kept his arm in place as he guided her down the hall once more.

Giuseppe was in the middle of some prep work, but immediately set it to the side when the duo walked in. "*Buongiorno,* Signore and Signorina Gismondi!"

After they returned his greeting, Agostino addressed the chef. "Giuseppe, could you please tell us if you have any seafood or aubergine planned on the menu?"

Giuseppe shook his head. "No, Signore. Not for the next week at least."

Agostino nodded. "Good. We'd like to ask you to permanently remove such items. My daughter is not fond of them."

"Consider it done, Signore."

After a quick "*grazie*", they let Giuseppe get back to his work in peace.

As they walked down another hallway, Adriana took in each and every painting and photograph that adorned the walls. For as long as she could remember, she had thought that living in a museum would be the greatest thing. She realized then that she practically was. She wondered if she would have appreciated the home as much, had she been able to grow up in it. She was pretty sure that the answer would be yes.

Her phone pinged the notification for a text message and Adriana was momentarily confused. She could not imagine who would be sending her a message and figured it must be a wrong number.

Agostino's phone pinged as well and his expression was amused. "It seems your brothers' have also gotten a late start on the day."

She took out her phone while Agostino looked at his. From the preview on the lock screen she could see the message began with, "*About what happened yesterday…*".

Agostino glanced over her shoulder. "That's Sergio's number."

Adriana felt slight knots form in her stomach, not sure what to expect, when she opened the message.

"*About what happened yesterday…I want to say I'm sorry. What I said was unfair and out of line. You didn't deserve to hear that. I hope you can forgive me.*"

"He's first apologizing to you, now?"

Agostino's tone snapped her out of her thoughts. "It… it probably just took him a while to figure out what exactly he wanted to say."

Agostino nodded, though his face was tinged with light skepticism. He seemed willing, though, to let the matter go, for the time being at least.

She turned back to her phone to write a quick reply. Adriana had never been prompt in returning messages, mostly because they were few and far between, but she thought keeping Sergio from stressing over a reply was the least she could do.

"All is forgiven."

She looked back at Agostino. "Did he send you a message as well?"

"No, it was from Ignacio. He said he was waiting to make sure we both were up." His expression was amused.

"You don't believe him, do you?"

Agostino chuckled. "Not for a single second."

She laughed at his answer and found herself wondering if Ignacio was like her, slow to wake up, even after leaving the bed. She then started wondering what else she had in common with her brothers.

He held out his hand. "Here, let me add everyone's number in for you. That way you can keep track of who is sending you what."

She went into the contact section of her phone and turned it over to him. As he worked, a thought struck Adriana. "How does Sergio know my number?"

Agostino briefly glanced up. "Macario shared it after you went to bed your first night home. He said it was the first thing they asked for, after we went to your room."

"What happened to my parents?" Unlike most five-year-old children trying to drag out bedtime, Adriana asked the question that had been on her mind for days. It was just in that moment she had plucked up the courage to ask.

"No one knows, honey." Her foster father gave her a soft look.

"Do you think they're out there, somewhere?"

"I wish we could tell you for sure." Sadness shone in her foster mother's eyes.

"Maybe I'll find them one day."

"If you do, we hope they're everything you deserve."

124

Over the coming months, she thought it might be okay to never find her birth family, as long as she could be a part of that one.

It was not meant to be though. Her foster mother fell ill, and even with the state support, they could not afford to keep her. She had no other choice than to go where they told her and hope it was as pleasant as the last place.

She was touched, to put it mildly, by how eager they were to make her a part of their lives. Growing up, she had often wondered if there was anyone out there who missed her even a little bit. As the phone pinged a few more times while Agostino worked, she realized the answer was a resounding yes. It took a bit of effort to keep her face even.

Agostino handed her phone back to her. "That should be sufficient for now. The number for your brothers, your sisters-in-law and myself are all in there now."

She gave him a grateful smile.

The day passed surprisingly quick for her. Lunch and dinner were pushed even later due to the late breakfast.

It was a short while after dinner, that she had to stifle a yawn. When she bid Agostino good night, he went for his office while she went for her room.

She was lying in bed, when she found the urge to look at the contacts in her phone. She was a bit confused when there was nothing under the A's section. She thought that Agostino had put his number in as well. Something made her scroll further down the list.

She realized why his number was not where she had expected it to be. Sitting right there between *Paola* and *Sergio*:

Papà

She closed her phone, then closed her eyes.

The Promises

Adriana was not sure what to do with her newfound free time. No bills to worry about, no cleaning that had to be done, no job to clock into. She had all the time in the world and no idea what to do with it. She and Agostino had spent the past couple of days together talking about everything and anything. When he tried to downplay a couple of work things that required his attention, she reassured him that it was perfectly fine that he tended to them. He eventually relented, and she had finally gotten an attention reprieve. She had opted to try to make some headway on her reading list. When she heard a noise by the door, Adriana looked up from her book, surprised to see Valentino strolling into the room. "Valentino, what are you doing here?" She put the book down and stood up.

His muscular arms immediately enveloped her in a huge hug. "I took the day off to spend some time alone with my sorellina."

She felt her heart swell. Adriana could not remember the last time someone had gone out of their way, just to spend time with her. "That's really sweet of you…"

He grabbed her hand and started leading her out of the room. "Come on! We're heading into town. I've already told Papà about it, so he can let Giuseppe know that you won't be here for lunch."

Valentino drove almost exactly like his older brother, so the trip into town was quick. She was almost getting used to it though. He parked on a street that led to the center.

After helping his sister out of the car, Valentino gave her his infectious grin. "You're going to show me all your favorite spots!"

Adriana became flustered. She had never really explored the town, since the plan had been that she would be there on a temporary basis. It was now a big regret for her as her mind raced to come up with a reasonable explanation. "As much as I hate to say it, aside from the pizzeria, I haven't really found any favorite spots. Getting here, getting settled in, getting the gallery up and running has taken up a lot of my time, so I haven't had so much of a chance to explore."

"You've got the time now, so let's walk around and see what catches your eye!"

She gave her brother a grateful smile and started to walk when he gestured ahead of them. He fell into step beside her.

When they reached the center, he headed towards the left. He pointed out various shops and told her which ones had good reputations and which ones bad.

At one point, he jabbed a finger accusingly towards a small café. "Whatever you do, never set foot in there."

She furrowed her brow. "What's wrong with it?"

Valentino scoffed. "Rumor has it they over roast their beans and it kills the flavor." His expression was one of pure disgust.

"Duly noted." She was slightly amused but mostly understanding in her brother's passion over coffee preparation.

They had been walking for around a kilometer when she took note of him shooting a death glare over her shoulder for the third time. She had been trying to ignore it, but found she could not. "Just what are you doing, Valentino?"

"No one has the right to look at my sorellina, the way that guy was."

Adriana rolled her eyes. "You do realize I'm almost thirty. I think I can handle an idiot on my own."

Valentino's face was completely serious and laced with traces of sadness. "The very first promise I ever made to you was that I would always protect you. Since I'm behind on that by almost several decades... I have a lot of catching up to do."

Her heart broke at his expression. It seemed so foreign yet so perfectly placed on his face. She stopped walking and turned him to face her. "None of that was your fault, Valentino!"

"I could have gone to the park with you that day. I could have drawn attention so you weren't taken."

She looked him directly in the eyes. As much as she wanted to push him for information on what exactly had happened, she knew it was not the time. "What if you had gotten taken as well? What then?"

Valentino ignored her question. "I should have been there to protect you, but I wasn't. I let you down and it's first now, I'm finally getting the chance to make it up to you."

She wrapped her arms around Valentino and held him tight. "I don't think you did anything wrong, but if you need to hear it, then I forgive you."

Her brother sighed with relief while he returned her embrace. "Thank you, sorellina. Thank you." His voice was barely above a whisper.

Her heart ached when she realized just how big of a cross he had bared over all of these many years. She could almost feel the burden being lifted. "You're welcome." Her own voice was equally as soft.

They started walking again, Valentino's arm still tightly wrapped around his little sister.

When they reached a green area, she spotted a group of orchids popping out of the ground. She thought them exquisite and she could not help herself as she bent down and sniffed them, the scent both intoxicating and comforting all at once. Adriana heard the click of Valentino's smartphone camera and swung her gaze over to him. "I hate having my picture taken!"

"Well, this one isn't too bad, if I do say so myself." He held the phone out to her.

Her eyes widened, as she took in the picture. It was a close-up of her face as she sniffed the flower. The fact that it had only taken him a few moments to capture such a shot amazed her. The lighting was perfect and the depth of field would have a lot of photographers green with envy. Even more than that though, he caught her emotion in the moment, shown by her closed eyes and the serene smile on her face. She actually adored the picture. "I think that's my most favorite picture anyone has ever taken of me!"

Valentino smiled softly. "It's my second favorite picture I've ever taken of you."

Adriana's brow furrowed. She could not recall any other opportunity he would have had. "What do you mean?"

Valentino cleared his throat. "The picture that's been on Papà's desk… that's my favorite."

Her eyes widened in shock. "Wait… you took that?"

Valentino nodded. "I do hope you'll let me take a lot more."

Adriana's head was still spinning. "But the picture on his desk... I was sure it was a professional shot... you were just a kid!"

He shrugged in response. "What can I say? I've always had a knack for it."

Adriana was still stunned. "Why did you get into finance then?"

Valentino laughed. "Well, a photographer's salary is hardly going to pay for a Maserati..."

She grabbed onto her brother's hand. "You can take as many pictures of me as you want."

"I'll definitely be taking you up on that, sorellina!"

He wasted no time on the unlimited picture taking. As he guided her through winding backstreets and side roads, he would tell her where to pose, every shot just as good as the first one. She had never felt like a model but she had to admit her brother made it easy.

Adriana's sense of navigation had never been strong so she had completely lost track of where in town they could possibly be, but she found she did not care. She was with her brother. That was all that mattered.

When they were walking past a jewelry shop, her eyes fell onto a rose gold locket sitting in the window. It was a large circle and ringed with glittering diamonds. She could not help the gasp that escaped her lips. Adriana did not even want to think how much it would set her back…she just wanted to imagine it around her neck. Granted she did have Agostino's credit card, but she did not feel right using it, despite what he said.

Valentino looked between her and the locket and grinned. He took hold of her hand and led his sister into the shop.

The small bell tinkered away as they stepped through the door. The woman sitting behind the counter got a large grin on her face, when she saw Valentino. "Signore Valentino! It's been so long! Here for something for Signora Esta?"

Valentino laughed. "Not this time, no. I'd actually like the locket in the front window. My sorellina is quite charmed by it."

Before she could voice her objections to Valentino- after all he had not even glanced at the price before deciding to buy it-the shop lady swept over to them.

"Signorina Gismondi… I've heard all the talk… please let me welcome you home."

Adriana was once more thrown by being addressed with that name. While Marie and Giuseppe had been calling her that, it had been in Agostino's home. Hearing it come from a woman whom she had just met, but who was wearing an expression of happiness and relief and endearment… could it be people she was not even related to had been worried about her all these years? Adriana did not know what to think so she threw on a smile instead. "Thank you very much."

"I'm sure you'll be coming in here a lot, sorellina. Bianca has the best jewelry store in town. Just ask any of your sisters-in-law."

Bianca laughed as she made her way over to the window, retrieving the locket. "Would you like this boxed or would you rather have it right away?"

She glanced quickly at Valentino. She could tell there was no point in trying to talk him out of buying it for her. "I'd like it now, please."

Bianca pulled the locket off the display stand and held it out for her.

She took it and looked over at her brother. "Could you help me get it on, please?"

Valentino nodded, pulling a credit card from his wallet and handing it over to Bianca before taking the necklace from his sister.

She turned her back to him, waiting until he reached around to pull her hair up. While he worked on the clasp, Adriana tried to not gasp when she saw the total on the cash register flash. Her brother had just dropped two thousand euro on her and he was acting like it was nothing more than buying her a ticket to the cinema. When she felt the necklace fall into place, she could not help but take a couple of steps towards the mirror on the counter. A soft smile broke on her face as she gazed at the reflection.

When Valentino stepped towards her, she spun around and stood on her tiptoes, and threw her arms around him. "Thank you so much!" Her hug was fierce.

"Get used to it, sorellina. From now on, what you want, you get."

They bid Bianca goodbye and continued down the street once more.

Valentino glanced at his watch and gave her a grin. "I know exactly where we're going to head to next."

After ten minutes of walking, the area started to look more and more familiar. Nervous knots formed in Adriana's stomach when she realized they were on the way to the pizzeria. She tried to push the thoughts from her mind.

When they reached the place, Adriana was momentarily surprised when Valentino stepped in first, rather than holding the door for her. She then remembered that a restaurant was the exception to the rule, as the man was expected to be the one to make the arrangements.

The employee, whom she knew as Massimo, grinned when he saw Valentino. "Signore Valentino!

It's been almost a week since we heard from you. We were getting worried!"

Valentino laughed in response. "I'll try my best to not let it happen again." He turned to his sister. "Do you have a usual?"

She gave him a slightly sheepish look and nodded.

He gave her a quick wink before turning back to Massimo. "My sorellina and I would like our usual, please."

Massimo's eyes widened ever so slightly as he put two and two together. To his credit, that was the only hint Massimo gave of his reaction. "Coming right up, Signore Valentino, Signorina Gismondi." He gave each a nod before he got to work.

They took a table close to the wall. The pizzeria was half-full and every now and then she would catch a quick glance and a soft whisper to a table companion and the frantic typing on a smartphone. Apparently, they had all heard what Massimo had called her.

Valentino tried to give her a reassuring smile. "I give it fifteen minutes, tops, before the whole town knows we're out and about today."

Adriana shifted in her seat, not sure how to handle the minor uproar she was causing.

Her brother clasped onto her hand as he cast a quick glance around the pizzeria. Valentino puffed himself out slightly as he locked eyes with his sister. "No one will bother us. I promise."

Adriana tried to downplay her discomfort. "I never had the desire to be a celebrity, even a minor one!"

"The whole thing will be over with soon enough. Then, people won't think twice about seeing you around town."

She found herself hoping he was right. She gave her brother a soft smile as their pizzas were delivered to their table.

A warm grin broke on her face when she realized they had the exact same pizza.

As they began to eat, a thought caused her to stare off into the distance.

"Something wrong with your pizza?" Valentino questioned.

"All this time…" her voice was quiet. "How many times in the past few months could our paths have crossed?"

Valentino's face was laced with regret. "Work has kept me busy as well. I'd usually send one of my assistants to get my lunch. I wish so many times over that I hadn't done that."

His sister gave him a soft smile. "You couldn't have known who I am."

Valentino's eyes locked with hers. "If you say so…"

She blinked rapidly, to keep the threatening tears at bay. She would give anything, to get that look off her brother's face. "There's what was, and there's what can be. That has to be the focus right now."

He only replied with a nod, his eyes brimming with emotion.

She reached out and gave him a reassuring squeeze, as much for herself as for him.

The staff wasted no time in sweeping their plates away when they were done.

"Since we're in the area, why don't we swing by your gallery and just confirm Bellissa has been taking good care of it? Not that I have any doubt that that is the case!"

Adriana felt daggers in her head and every other part of her body. She had been a champion in avoidance the last few days. She wondered if she could continue it. "That sounds great!" Adriana hoped she was being a lot more convincing than she felt.

It took all of ten seconds for the road to clear for them to cross.

Adriana could feel the knot in her stomach tighten as they approached her gallery. Everything she had been trying to put out of her mind came rushing forward.

"I'm just trying to give you a realistic perspective."

Adriana gritted her teeth. Less than three years to go and she'd be aging out of the system and she would not have to endure these meetings any longer. She had lost track of how many social workers had come before, but Adriana knew for sure this was one she liked the least.

"There's no paper trail for you to go off of. Of course, you can do as you like when you turn eighteen. I can't stop you. But the chances of you finding biological family is highly unlikely."

"You've just said, no one knows anything about them, so you can't say anything about them with certainty."

"Adriana...they've had all these years. Why haven't they tried to find you, if they're still out there?"

"They're could be any number of reasons! Just because you've seen it a lot, doesn't make it fact!"

The social worker's face became hard. "Look, the sooner you accept the fact that your biological family most likely wants nothing to do with you, the better off you'll be."

Adriana felt her heart break but she forced her face to stay even. "IF that should be the case, I'll handle it then. If not, I'll happily come back and tell you just how damn wrong you are!"

Bellissa was finishing up on the phone when Valentino and his sister walked in. She waved at the duo, smiling as she hung up. She was around Adriana's height and her thick, blonde braid fell almost all the way down her back. "Well hello, you two!" Her cornflower blue eyes were full of excitement.

Valentino and Bellissa quickly embraced before she turned her full attention to her sister-in-law. "I'm Bellissa, Ignacio's wife. I'm so happy to get to tell you welcome home." Not being able to contain herself, Bellissa reached out and drew her in for a tight hug. "My husband's been the happiest the past few days that I can ever remember him being. Thank you for that."

If there was ever a time in Adriana's life that she felt she did not deserve to be thanked, it was that moment. "You're welcome," she whispered. "I really appreciate you covering for me. I'll try not to be too much longer."

"Take all the time you need! I'm a freelancer, so I can do a lot of my regular work from here. There's no rush at all."

She nodded and gave her sister-in-law an appreciative smile.

140

The time she and Valentino were there was a blur for Adriana as the conflict inside of her grew with every passing minute. They were no longer pieces of paper and accusations. They were living, breathing people who would be affected by what she did.

She did her best to not seem distracted the rest of the afternoon as Valentino continued to show her around but Adriana could not keep the thoughts from flying around her head. She did not even note Valentino's driving on the way home.

She bid Valentino goodbye with a tight hug and made her way to Agostino's office. She knocked lightly on the door.

He looked up from his paperwork, shutting the file as he rose. His smile was large. "Did you have a good day with your brother?"

She nodded. Amongst the thoughts that had been whirling through her head, there was something that she thought could help her, even if she could not explain why. "There's actually a favor, I have to ask of you."

Agostino made his way around the desk. "Of course, *tesorino mio,* whatever you need."

She indicated the necklace. "Valentino... he got this for me today. I... I was hoping I could get a picture of my mother, to put in it."

Agostino smiled softly, and he made his way back to his desk. He pulled open the top drawer and took out a picture. His gaze was trained on it for several long moments before he held it out to her.

When she took it, her mouth formed a small "o". The picture was of the newborn her, with her mother's nose pressed to her forehead. She had to have been only a few minutes old. The look of complete and utter love on her mother's face nearly took her breath away. Her eyes flew up to Agostino's. "I… I can't take this one. I can't cut it up!"

Agostino's smile was laced with sadness. "It is not the only one. I have the negatives, and would have one printed off every year, just in case it was the year I found you again." His gaze was completely endearing. "You look so much like her you know."

She stared down at the picture. Yes, she did look a great deal like her mother. But there was one thing that was not a perfect match. She lifted her gaze and was almost ready to kick herself for not realizing it sooner. The eyes that met hers were a perfect reflection of her own. "Everything except the eyes…" her voice dropped off.

Agostino cupped her cheek with his hand. "Yes. Your brothers all got their eyes from your mother, but I was finally able to pass mine on to you."

She fought the torrent of emotions that were storming through her.

142

"One of the very last promises I made to your mother was that all of you would have amazing lives. I can't even begin to say how relieved I am to finally be able to keep that promise to her."

"I know," she whispered softly. "I'll see you at dinner."

Agostino planted a long kiss on her forehead, then headed back around his desk.

She wandered the halls, not having any idea where she wanted to go. She stopped in the middle of the hallway and leaned up against a door.

She lifted the picture of her mother and her and stared at it, burning the image into her mind. If there was indeed life after death, what was her mother thinking of what she had been up to? Was she enraged or understanding or disapproving? Is it something her mother would or could or both forgive her for?

"I'm so, so sorry," she whispered at the picture.

The Photographs

Adriana was back in the library once more. This time it was a photo album that she was looking at. She needed to understand the full implications her decision would have, so she could make the right one. Agostino had shown her a photo the night before. It was one of all of her nieces and nephews. He had told her that they were all looking forward to meeting her, when she was ready. Adriana's sense of guilt took over and she had agreed to a party, to be held the following weekend. Bellisa's words echoed in her head, and she wondered if that was also the case for her other brothers. What sort of impact would that have on their children? What would it be like for them to see their father's and grandfather's heart get broken again?

She put the album back on the shelf and grabbed another one, further back. Adriana sat down on the couch and opened it, studying each photo intently. She almost did not notice her eldest brother come into the library.

"There you are!" Macario exclaimed. "It took forever to track you down!" He gave her a kiss and hug, before taking a seat next to her on the couch. "What are you doing?"

"Just looking through some of the photos," Adriana replied, doing her best to sound casual. She could not help but feel a bit of shame. She hoped Macario did not notice.

He looked down at the photo. "That's one from my twelfth birthday." He smiled, sweet memories clearly rushing into his head. "Papà made the cake." Macario said as he pointed it out in the picture.

"Really?"

Macario nodded. "He's going to be so happy to not have to guess at yours this year."

"What do you mean?"

"Every year, he'd bake a cake on your birthday. It always bothered him that he wasn't sure if it was one you would like or not."

"Every year?" Her voice was tinged with disbelief. A cake made from scratch on her birthday was something she had never experienced. In a way, Agostino doing that did not even surprise her and somehow it made her feel even more ashamed.

Macario explained the story behind each photo and each one tugged at her heartstrings. She soaked up each and every story.

When they reached the end, Macario selected another photo album, a few spots behind the one they were just looking at.

He sat down next to his sister and opened the album. She stifled a gasp when she realized the first picture was the same one that sat right above her heart.

There were dozens of photos at the hospital but the one that got to her the most was Agostino holding her up so she was eye level with him. They were in front of a window and sunlight streamed through but it looked dull in comparison to his smile.

Macario turned the page. "This was when you first came home from the hospital." Macario's grin was large. "Mamma had threatened to not let any of us hold you because we kept fighting over who would get to be the first. I eventually won, when I made the argument that I had been waiting the longest for a baby sister."

"You knew your calling at a very early age."

"What about you? When did you figure out paintings are your passion?"

"From the first time I set foot in a museum." A large smile was on her face. "Paintings… they give a sense of what life was like, what was important in a way that no history book can. They give an idea of the passions, of the dreams, of the trials that people faced and how they overcame or fell to them. So much of the subject matter, the heart of it, is so relevant today and it can inspire, or it can warn, if people just take a minute to look deeper at them."

"You're late." A smiled played on the face of the woman behind the counter.

"Sorry, Peggy. Missed the bus this week."

"Well, you made it after all. That's what matters."

When Adriana went to hand her a couple of bills the woman waved it off. "Don't worry about it this week. Don't try arguing with me about it, I'm not changing my mind!" She held out the ticket with a big smile. "You have application fees you need to think about soon."

"Promise you'll keep your fingers crossed for me?"

"Nope, I won't. Because you don't need any luck."

"Thanks, Peggy."

Adriana went about her usual route throughout the museum. The consistency and stability was one of the only things that was helping her survive her last year in the system. Despite what Peggy had said, she felt she needed all the luck she could get. The statistics for kids that aged out of the system becoming successful were far from optimistic. Looking at the paintings, renewed her faith in herself, that there was still some hope for her.

Each painting she stopped at, she studied it for what felt like the first and the millionth time. Months ago, she had started making up stories to go with each painting. She played each and every story in her head. Some were happy, some were sad. There were those with great conflicts while others were about simple misunderstandings. The same stories would lull her to sleep every night.

She knew she should be saving every penny from her allowance to cover the cost of applying to university, but she would sacrifice everything else, before she would sacrifice these visits. The paintings were more than pretty pictures to her. They were her lifeline, her reason to continue to fight when she felt like it was all too much.

Her story had an uncertain beginning and she was terrified of having an uncertain ending.

Adriana finally stopped, blushing slightly. "I'm sorry. I'm rambling."

"Not at all! Please, continue."

It was the genuineness on his face that got to her the most. He was truly interested in what she had to say, and it caused her face to break out into an even larger smile. "The history and evolution of it is also fascinating! Starting from parietal art up into the present day, the changing of mediums, of techniques, of subject matter to convey a message is one of the richest histories of all, for me at least."

Her brother grinned at her. "I'm looking forward to you teaching me everything you know!"

"I am as well."

Macario turned the page and pointed to the picture in the upper left corner. "See, there we are!"

She took in everything about the picture as she did with all the ones that followed. Each of her brothers had indeed gotten a turn to hold her. Even Sergio had, by way of sitting on their mother's lap. She was at a loss for words when they got to the end and she realized all of the pictures were from her first month of life.

"I know which one we should take next." Her brother grabbed an album on the far side of the set.

His sister's curiosity was piqued. When Macario opened it, she saw Agostino and Rosalia's wedding picture, the one she had spotted in the hallway the other day. Before she could say anything though, he turned the page. The sight that greeted her was Agostino and Rosalia in the exact same pose, the only difference being the clothing and Macario being in their mother's arms. The next one the same pose, Macario in Agostino's arms and Valentino in Rosalia's. The next one, same pose, Agostino and Macario, Rosalia and Valentino and Dante and so on and so on. One for every year of marriage until it ended with Rosalia with Sergio and a baby her, Agostino with Constantin and Ignacio, and Macario, Valentino, and Dante standing in front of them.

"It was Mamma's idea," her brother's voice broke through her thoughts. "She wanted all of us to see just how much their love grew over time."

"That's … amazing." She could barely hear her own voice.

When he flipped the page, there were four newborn photos on one page and three on the other.

He pointed to the picture in the upper right corner of the left page. "Guess which of our brothers, that is." Macario said with a grin.

She was much too distracted to consider any sort of chronological order to the photos. The baby did seem on the smaller side, at least in comparison to the others. "Sergio?" She gave her best guess.

"That's Valentino, actually."

"What?!" She could not keep the shock from her voice.

Macario smiled at her reaction. "The only one of us who was smaller than him, was you."

She was grateful for the small distraction from her heavy thoughts, so Adriana said the first thing that came to her mind. "And I thought Constantin had an appetite!"

Her brother threw his head back and laughed. "It was when we saw how tiny you were, that you became 'sorellina' to us. It wouldn't matter how old you got, you were always going to be our baby sister."

"So that's the story behind that."

He wasted no time in pulling another album down from the shelf. "Here's one you have to see."

"What is it?" His expression intrigued her.

"Your baptism." He took his spot on the couch again and opened the album.

A quick glance told her it was rather thick and Adriana furrowed her brow. "Wait. Is the entire album full of pictures from that day?"

Macario merely nodded. He pointed to the first picture, which was set in the center of the page. "Here's you and Mamma."

Her mouth hung open slightly as she looked at the picture. She was wearing a white satin gown with a pink bow tied around, and she was in her mother's arms. Rosalia's smile was shining. "Our mother was there…?"

Macario rubbed her shoulder. "Mamma had started not feeling well shortly before but she wouldn't let anything make her miss that day." He cleared his throat and turned the page. "This one is you and Papà."

She took a closer look at the picture. Agostino could not have looked prouder as he cradled her in his arms. He looked like he had found the most valuable treasure in the world and was showing it off to everyone.

The next picture was her mother standing with them, and the one after that was all of her brothers, in their little suits, standing around them. Each picture burrowed deep into her heart.

"These are your godparents, Zio Edmondo and Zia Vittoria. They're Papà's brother and sister. The man standing with them is Father Vozzella."

"I have godparents?" Her voice was a half whisper.

Macario nodded as he continued onto the next page. He started listing off the various people in the pictures. It seemed like every last relation had had their picture taken with her that day.

Her head was swimming from the numerous names of various aunts and uncles and cousins. Part of her was in a bit of shock that such a big deal would be made over her. If she was lucky when she was growing up, she would get a practical gift like socks on her birthday. When she saw a picture that had a table full of presents in the background, she was almost certain it was more gifts than she had ever gotten in her life. The impact it had on her, had less to do with material possessions and more to do with the sheer number of people who gave a damn about her.

"I just need a minute." Adriana hastily stood up, grabbed her cigarettes and lighter, and headed for the door.

Her lighter was not working properly and after several tries, her cigarette was still unlit.

"Here." Her brother was standing by her, holding out his butane lighter, which was aflame.

She gave him a small smile. "*Grazie.*" When her cigarette was lit, she pulled back and took a long drag.

Macario pulled out his own pack of cigarettes, lighting one for himself. "I'm sorry, sorellina. I didn't mean to upset you."

"It's not your fault." She tried to reassure him. "It just... caught me off guard."

"We weren't as happy as we could have been."

"That's not it ... I can't and I don't begrudge any of you the happy times ... I just feel ... robbed."

"So do we."

She tossed her cigarette in the ashtray and wrapped her arms around her brother. It took him only moments to follow suit.

"I have a confession to make to you. When Mamma and Papà would go to bed, I'd sneak into your room and sleep on the floor."

"Why would you do that?"

"Because if something made you upset, I wanted to make it better. Don't get me wrong, it was only less than a minute or two before one of them would be in... but for me, it was too long to make you wait. They'd send me back to bed but, after a few nights, they gave up trying to get me not to sneak in, in the first place."

"You were just a kid..." Her voice was barely above a whisper.

"It's always been my part in the family. While Papà is one of the strongest people we'll probably ever know, after Mamma passed and you were taken ... there were times when the darkness became too much for him ... it was up to me to hold it all together for everyone. When those times passed and I could let go a bit, I'd go lay in your room. Papà would update it every few years. I'd imagine that you were there and could comfort you just like when you were a baby. It helped give me strength."

Adriana was pretty sure she knew how a bullet through the gut felt. The way he spoke with such emotion about her had her heart screaming. She had always been a part of their lives, even without being there.

She was also processing everything her brother had just said about Agostino. All the files she had read had made Agostino seem like a complete monster but everything she had seen, heard and experienced had been screaming that that was not the case. Bureau intelligence was far from infallible. Maybe the reason no one had been able to find anything was because there was nothing to find. That had to be a possibility. She turned her focus back to her brother. "You shouldn't have had to bear that burden."

"If it meant this, I'd do it a thousand times over."

She did not need to see his face to know there were tears. Her arms wrapped even tighter around her brother.

Neither were sure exactly how long they stood there like that, but neither really cared.

"Just so you know, Francesca has decided that we're going to be the first to arrive for the party. Ciana and I will hear about it for years if that isn't the case."

His sister softly smiled. "Has she already started a countdown?"

"Almost down to the second."

"I'm sorry that it won't be sooner. I just think that meeting them all at the same time is the fairest and I want just a little more time."

"It's perfectly fine, sorellina! If there is one thing Ciana and I are used to, it's dealing with our headstrong daughter. If we can survive the two-month long kitten campaign, we can survive anything!"

His sister lightly laughed. There was something about the expression on his face. "Why do I have the feeling she eventually won at the end?"

"Two months! We held out for two months! That's the focus of the story!"

Her laughter grew and Macario reluctantly joined her.

Agostino stepped out at that moment. "What's so funny, you two?" His eyes moved between his children.

For some reason, she only laughed more and had to gasp out the answer between laughs. "Macario ... he was ... just telling me ... about his failed ... kitten campaign resistance!"

Agostino joined them in laughter. He looked at his eldest child. "I told you from the beginning you were going to give in eventually."

"I know, I know." Macario's expression showed he had somehow managed to delude himself into thinking otherwise.

Agostino clasped onto his son's shoulder. "She fought for what was important for her and would not be dissuaded. She's just like you in that respect. You should be proud of that."

A soft smile graced her face as she took in her brother's grateful expression. No one could ever doubt how much Agostino's children meant to him. Was that

156

not the most important thing, when all was said and done?

Agostino turned his attention to her. "I just wanted to let you know that I've shortlisted three potential drivers for you. I'll be interviewing them in the next couple of days. Of course, you'll have the final word on which one we hire. You're welcome to partake in the interviews if you so wish."

Before she could think, the words spilled out of her mouth. "Bellissa did tell me that there's no rush, so we can take our time with that."

He smiled and nodded. "I just wanted to let you know. I'll let you two get back to what you were doing."

Before Agostino could even start to turn, she spoke. "We we're just looking through some of the photo albums. Why don't you join us?"

A wide smile broke on his face. "I'd be delighted."

When they were inside again, Macario gave his father a smile. "I haven't shown her yours and Mamma's wedding album yet. Why don't we take that one?"

"An excellent idea!" Agostino praised. He wasted no time in retrieving the album.

When Agostino sat down on the couch, she took the spot next to him and Macario the spot next to her. Agostino held the album between the two of them, so Macario could look on as well.

Every single picture showed just as much love and happiness as the first picture she saw and there was no doubt in her mind, that the camera had nothing to do with it. Their love for each other was as pure and as genuine as it got.

Something crossed her mind and made her curious. She remembered what Valentino had said before the dinner, about their mother being from Southern Italy. While it was not impossible, she found herself wanting to know just how their paths had come to cross. "How did you two meet?"

Agostino's expression was full of sentimental sweetness. "It's a funny little story actually. I had always had a favorite café, one that I would go to exclusively. There was one day though that I was between meetings on the other side of town and didn't have the time to go over there. I grudgingly went into the café nearby and it turned out to be the best decision I ever made."

"How so?"

"When I walked into the café, I saw your mother for the first time. She was nearly done with her coffee when our eyes met. I bought her another cup and she told me she was travelling and was only supposed to be in town that day. Well, needless to say that one day turned into many happy years."

"If you had had time to go by your usual café ... if your first meeting had lasted just a little bit longer ... if she had gotten to the café just a little bit earlier..."

There was a tender smile on Macario's face. "That is exactly the same thing we all said. As they always told us, that's how they knew they were meant to be."

She was struck by the thought of how, in a bizarre way, the only error she had ever made on the job ended up leading her back here. She had always been undecided about destiny but now she was almost certain, between Agostino and Rosalia's story, and her own situation, that it did indeed exist. All of her choices throughout her life; studying art, studying Italian, getting a job with the Bureau, losing their trust, getting sent here- it all led her back home. There was no way she could ever betray them, she was sure of it.

What she was not sure of, was if they could ever forgive her.

The Choices

Adriana was sitting at the table waiting on Dante. He
had invited her to lunch but had sent her a message a
short while ago, saying he had been delayed. He told
her he had already reserved a table so she could just say
she was meeting him so she did not have to stand
around waiting. Agostino had had some errands in
town, so he had just dropped her off on his way.

Dante walked up. He gave her a peck on the cheek
before sitting down. "Sorry for being late, sorellina."

"I thought being late was a requirement of
doctors."

Dante merely shook his head, clearly having heard
that all before.

Adriana jumped ever so slightly when her phone
pinged the notification for a text message. Another
quickly followed and then another. She took a glance at
her phone, confirming what she already knew-that there
were ten messages waiting for her in the past hour.
While every day had been like that, it still had not
become the norm for her. Adriana also felt a stab of
shame with each ping, knowing what she had been
ready to do to them all.

Dante gave her a gentle look. "So how have you
been handling everything, sorellina?"

"I should have put my phone to silent. I'm sorry for forgetting that," she apologized as she did just that. "You know, you're the first one to actually ask me that."

"Our family can be rather... enthusiastic, so to say." The expression on his face was one of patience. "Now, how about you stop avoiding my question? After all, there's no wrong answer."

While she was grateful for it, Adriana was finding his patience to be rather irritating, as well as his perception to what she had been trying to do. "I've been okay."

"Sorellina..."

It was the concern in his eyes that got to her the most. She had to tell him something and decided a half-truth would be best. "Sometimes, it's a bit much for me. Don't misunderstand me, please. Getting to know you all has been wonderful. It's just... in some of the foster homes I was in... I would be lucky if they said good morning to me. And after that, I've pretty much been on my own. So, to go from that to constant communication throughout the day..." She trailed off.

Dante reached across the table and took her hand in his. "If you need more time, or if you want to take things more slowly, just say the word and I'll make sure it happens."

"I just know how happy everyone has been… I don't want to be a disappointment."

Dante squeezed her hand. "You could never be a disappointment to us, sorellina. You shouldn't ever feel that there's anything you have to hide from us."

Adriana felt like a rock had been dropped in her stomach. *If you only knew,* she thought. "As long as I have you to talk to about it, I think I'll be okay."

"That you will always have, sorellina. I promise you."

She gave him a grateful smile. She picked up the menu, giving it a glance over. "So, what do you recommend here?"

"The risotto alla parmigiana and pasta al ragù has always been my favorite."

"That sounds good to me." She closed the menu and set it on the table.

Within seconds, the waitress came over to them. "What would you like today, Signore Dante and Signorina Gismondi?"

The reaction she had gotten when she said she was meeting her brother, Dante Gismondi, was almost exactly like how Massimo had reacted when she and Valentino were at the pizzeria; widened eyes and a sense of deference. As reluctant as she was to admit it, she did get a bit of a thrill from it. It was not entirely her fault though. Her family was obviously very well-respected in town and she could hardly be faulted for whom she was born to. She took a sip of her wine, while Dante placed their order.

When the waitress left, Dante picked up his own glass, which she had taken the liberty of ordering for him and held it towards his sister. "*Cin cin.*"

"*Cin cin*," she replied, clinking her glass with his.

"Natala and the children are very much looking forward to the party."

"Elena and Matteo, right?" She looked hopeful. She had been trying to learn everyone's name. Every day she studied the picture of her nieces and nephews and did her best to review who was who.

"Very close." His expression was one of tenderness. "Matteo is my son but my daughter is Elisa. Elena is Valentino's oldest."

Adriana sighed and looked away. "I knew that."

"Sorellina." Dante once more demonstrated his infinite patience and waited until she finally looked back at him. His behavior had made it clear that he could wait hours and the uncomfortable silence got to her. "No one is expecting you to have memorized the entire family tree in so short a time."

"That's just it, though." She distracted herself with her wine while the waitress placed the plates of risotto on the table. She waited until the waitress had departed before she continued. "I shouldn't have to be learning everyone's names. I should have known all of the kids from the moment they were born. I should have known all of your wives from the moment you all started dating them. I should have so many stories to tell the kids of the ridiculous things you all did at their age but I don't and it... and it..." She found she could not continue. The tears in her eyes made it almost impossible for her to speak.

Dante moved to the chair next to her and took her in his arms. His chin rested on top of her head, while one arm draped across her back and his other hand cradled the back of her head. "It feels like there's a giant hole in your heart." While his voice was quiet, she was still able to hear the pain in it, despite his attempt to cover it.

"Yes," she whispered.

"We never stopped worrying and we never stopped hoping."

"How did it happen? Please, I need to know."

Dante began to rock her, ever so slightly. "Mamma had fallen ill, and Papà needed help with all of us. He hired two nannies-one for us and one for you. After she passed, he decided to keep them on, on a more permanent basis. Fourteen days after we laid Mamma to rest, your nanny took you to the park. It was the first nice day all year. The sun was shining and the trees

164

were starting to bud and she thought it would be good for you and Papà agreed. When you and her were in a more remote area, she was attacked by two men. By the time she came to, you and her attackers were gone. The police were contacted immediately, but your nanny couldn't give a clear description, as they had caught her off guard. The search began but it was figured the men had a half hour head start and were most likely not going to be staying in town. Even the national police forces were pulled in but they weren't able to pick up any trail."

"Were the men ever found?" She could barely hear her own voice.

"No. If they had been, we had no doubts we would have been able to find you." He took a deep breath as he held her tighter. "We won't give up until we find who was behind it, though. I swear it."

"Was there any idea as to why they took me?"

"No, there isn't. Whether it was a matter of chance or something more malicious … we will one day find out, if we have anything to say about it."

"Somebody might have wanted us all to suffer?"

Dante seemed to take his time, choosing his words carefully. "It is a possibility, not a certainty."

"Why?"

"I can't say, sorellina. What I do know is that people said you were the only thing that got Papà through the funeral. Though the same was true for the rest of us."

She bit back a moan. How she could have thought she was capable of ripping their hearts out again, she did not know.

"A few of Papà's brothers, they are on the police force. They always kept their ears and eyes open, just in case they came across something that might lead us to you."

There was something that had been nagging at her for a while, and she figured now was as good of a time as any to ask. "What about our mother's family?"

Dante took a deep breath. "We don't have any contact with them. When Mamma first started dating Papà, her family didn't approve. When she told them they were getting married, they gave her an ultimatum. It was them or him. None of them were at the wedding and none of us have even met them."

"How could they have made her do that?"

"I don't know, sorellina. Sometimes, the family one has, is a choice that one has to make."

Somehow, his words sent a shiver down her spine. She hoped he did not notice.

When she realized he was not going to let go until she did, she pulled back and cast a hasty glance around the restaurant. Adriana was embarrassed to have a breakdown in a public place but to their credit, the few other patrons in the restaurant made a point of not looking in her and Dante's general direction. "I'm sorry. I'm sure this wasn't what you were expecting when you invited me to lunch."

"Expectations are something I've never bothered with. I'm just glad you came out with these things, no matter the place. Keeping all those emotions bottled up- it won't make for anything good."

Her smile was sad. "I would have been able to come to you with anything, wouldn't I?"

"You still can, sorellina."

Part of her was screaming for her to tell him the complete and utter truth right then and there, but Adriana did not dare risk it. Even if they could forgive her for not knowing who she was when she first took the assignment, she could not honestly say that she was willing to drop it the second she found out the truth. She had been ready to betray them all and if they found that to be unforgivable, they might just cut her off and she could not handle that. "I'll remember that," she said with a whisper.

When they finished with lunch, Dante paid and they stepped out. They were only a little way down the street when she caught of whiff of something that made her sigh with pleasure, despite the scrumptious meal she had just had.

Dante's eyes went between his sister at the cart on the corner of the street, a smile on his face. "Say no more." He went for the cart and she fell into step beside him.

"Two orders of zeppole, please."

The man at the cart filled two paper bags and handed them to Dante. He passed one over to her as they made their way towards the large fountain.

She ate one, savoring the delicious sweetness. "I have had to exercise so much self-control to only get these once a week."

Dante smiled softly. "Funny enough, that was Papà and Mamma's rule for us. It became a Friday tradition after Macario started school. We'd be with when Mamma picked him up and the first stop was the zeppole cart. The rule was one order each, the exception being her when she was pregnant. She'd get two-one for herself and one for the baby, as she always said."

There was a brief hesitation before she spoke. She was not sure if what she was about to say would be seen as ridiculous, given that they were all adults, but she could not help herself. "Maybe one Friday soon, if you all have the time … we could meet up for some zeppole."

168

Dante cupped her face. "We will make the time."

His sister gave him a grateful smile.

"There's something I have to confide in you, sorellina."

"What is it?"

"Ignacio had told me, how he had told you about our summer nights under the stars." When she nodded, Dante continued. "When everyone would fall asleep, I'd sneak back into the house and take two extra sleeping bags out and put them on either side of me and pretend you and Mamma were there with us."

Tears sprang into her eyes as she wrapped her arms around her brother. "I've missed you so much. Even if I didn't know exactly what it was, I was missing, I did."

"We missed you, too. More than we will ever be able to say. There wasn't a second that went by that we didn't."

"We don't have to worry about that anymore." She hoped with every fiber of her being that what she said would be the truth.

On the drive home, Dante did prove to be the most conservative of her brothers so far, with regards to driving, though that was not saying very much.

Right before they had left town, she went back to the cart and got an extra order of zeppole. She had wrapped the bag tight, hoping it would hold as much freshness as possible.

Agostino was walking out of his office as she approached and that special smile he seemed to always have with her broke out on his face. "Did you two have a good lunch?"

She nodded and held the bag up for him. "I brought these for you. Dante told me that it was a Friday tradition but I figured they would still taste as good."

Agostino cupped her face when he took the bag. "*Tesorino mio*, you are so thoughtful."

The next words came tumbling out, before she could stop them. "He told me something else … he told me … how it happened."

He nodded. "I know I had promised to tell you the whole story one day and I'm sorry that I didn't. Me agreeing with your nanny's suggestion has haunted me every single second since. You coming home is the only thing that has given me a bit of a reprieve."

Her voice was filled with conviction. "What happened is not your fault!"

"There are acres of trees and fresh air right here! There is no reason to have taken you into town for that." It was painfully clear that it was a logic that had gone through Agostino's mind so many times, it had been burned into his brain.

"You had no reason to think that what happened was even a remote possibility! You can't blame yourself!"

"I beg to differ with you." His voice was quiet.

She did the only thing she could and wrapped her arms tight around him. "I don't and I won't blame you, no matter what."

It was not possible for Agostino to hold her closer. "They're not going to get away with what they did to us. I swear it with all my heart."

She found herself sincerely hoping that he was right.

The Gifts

Adriana found herself greatly needing distraction. Agostino's words of guilt from the other day were still flitting around her head, and she wanted to not think about it, if only for a little while. One of the many rooms in the house held an exquisite grand piano and while she was a bit rusty, Adriana thought it would make for a sufficient enough diversion from heavy thoughts.

Adriana let out a frustrated sigh when she tried to play the bridge for the eighth time and she failed yet again.

Constantin came strolling into the room. "That's always been one of my favorites!" He sat down next to his sister. His fingers deftly swept over the keyboard, easily playing the notes she had just been struggling with.

She shot him a look. "Show off."

Constantin threw his head back and laughed. "I just won't say how many months that took me to be able to do."

"How long have you been playing for?"

"Over a quarter of a century. I started when I was around eight."

"Okay, I feel better now. You've had about three times as long as me. I had my first lesson when I was at university."

Constantin nodded his approval. "That's actually pretty impressive, sorellina. From what I heard, I would have thought it was longer."

She was not aware of it, but she sat up a bit straighter, proud that she could make him proud. "So, what brings you by today?"

"Aside from seeing your wonderful self…I've sold a couple of Papà's properties and needed him to sign off on them. But, now that that's done, so I've got the rest of the afternoon for you."

"That's really sweet of you."

"Actually, I have something I've been meaning to give you." He reached into his pocket and pulled out a square, black velvet box and held it out to his little sister.

"What's this for?" She reached for the box, her curiosity piqued.

"Open it and you'll see."

She did as he said and when she opened the box, she found a silver charm bracelet with over a couple of dozen charms on it. At a glance, she could spot a piano, a horse, a bike and a pair of shoes. She gave Constantin a quizzical look.

His expression was wistful. "Each charm is something we could have been doing together every year. If you had wanted to do those things, of course," he said sheepishly.

His sister was at a loss for words. "Constantin…. that's…. the sweetest thing," she trailed off.

"It was Mamma's idea. Well sort of. When we came to see you two in the hospital, I started talking about all the things I was going to do with my baby sister. She told me to make a picture of all the things I wanted to do. When I got older, I decided to make the drawings something more permanent."

She gave him a confused look. "But you told me you're a horrible drawer, like me."

Constantin smiled softly. "Those were my exact words to Mamma. She told me it didn't matter if it didn't make sense to anyone else, as long as it made sense to me."

Adriana looked down and when she spoke, her voice was quiet. "I really don't deserve this…"

"Don't be silly, sorellina. Of course, you do!" He took the bracelet from her and clasped it around her right wrist.

She made herself look up at him and she smiled. "Thank you."

174

"Maybe we can take a look through and see if there isn't a couple of things we can manage to do. If not, we'll find things to do together."

"I would love that," she replied and she realized she meant it. Before all of the worrying thoughts that had been preoccupying Adriana's mind could take over, she had to change the subject. "Though you do know how high you've set the bar in the gift giving department, don't you?"

Her attempt at switching to something less emotional was a complete failure though. Constantin smiled. "At least the pile of Christmas gifts won't go to waste this year."

"What do you mean?"

"Every year, Papà would have a pile of presents waiting for you, in case you came home that year."

She felt her heart swell. There was no way she could have even the smallest doubt that Agostino had never given up on her. To mean that much to someone had always been a dream of hers and now that it was a reality, she wanted nothing more than to cling to it. "That sounds like something he would do."

Constantin nodded. "We'd sneak some in too…."

Adriana hesitated, but she had to ask him something. "If you don't want to talk about this, I'll understand, but…. can you tell me what happened to our mother? I know what Sergio said-"

He gently cut her off. "Sergio doesn't know what he's talking about." Constantin paused before continuing. "Dante's a better one to ask if you want lots of details but, it was due to a careless doctor. You were her seventh child. She said she was used to it at that point. But the doctor who examined her after…he was distracted and he ended up passing on an infection to her. By the time it was caught…it was too far gone to do anything."

"One person doing one stupid thing is why she isn't here with us right now?" She felt a mix of emotions rushing through her.

Constantin nodded.

Adriana looked off into the distance. "At the same time though, she wouldn't have been in the hospital in the first place, if it wasn't for me…"

Her brother took her chin between his fingers and turned her head towards him, a dead serious expression on his face. "You are in no way guilty of what happened to Mamma, got it? There is only one person who's to blame in that, and that was the doctor. I don't want to hear you ever try to take any blame again, okay?"

"Okay." She whispered, hoping she was being a lot more convincing than she felt. "I just hope he hasn't been allowed to practice medicine since then."

"He didn't."

Something about Constantin's tone and his use of the past tense made her feel a little foolish for thinking that Agostino would not have done something to the man responsible for his beloved wife's death. She was not sure how exactly she felt about it. She thought that she should probably be appalled, but she found that she could not be. If her mother had been around, she may have never been separated from her family in the first place.

In an effort to distract herself from the torrent of emotions that were coursing through her, she turned her attention back to the charm bracelet. She pointed to one which was a high heel shoe and a man's shoe joined at the heel. "What's this one for?"

"That is for ballroom dancing."

"You know how to dance?"

"Yes, I took some lessons back in my younger days." At his sister's dubious expression, Constantin laughed and continued. "To be perfectly honest, I started it because Valentino and I were having a competition for who could get the most dates in two months. We tried getting Dante into it but he said he was too busy being responsible." Constantin scoffed.

She rolled her eyes but at the same time, she found it oddly endearing.

"After the first month, I found out I was actually pretty good at it and I was having a great time, so I continued. That's how I ended up meeting the last girl I would ever date."

"So, a brotherly competition led to you meeting the love of your life?" She was in a bit of a marvel at that.

Constantin nodded. "From the moment I asked Paola to partner up with me, I knew she was the one for me."

"Teach me to dance," she said before she could stop herself.

"With pleasure," Constantin grinned. He took hold of her hand and pulled her up. "Now the first thing to remember is to keep your back straight." He pushed on the small of her back ever so slightly. "There, perfect. Now relax your shoulders… exactly!

"We'll start with a basic waltz. That's usually the easiest place to start."

She nodded, even though she was nervous. "I'm giving you fair warning; your feet might suffer for this."

"Sorellina, I have three children, another on the way, and a temperamental, perpetually pregnant wife who loves her high heels. You stepping on my foot

178

wouldn't be the worst thing it's encountered by far! Just follow my lead. We'll start off nice and slow, okay?"

True to his word, he led her through the steps, going in slow motion. When she seemed to have a feel for it, he picked up the pace ever so slightly. He did this a couple of times, until they were doing something resembling a dance.

"See, you're a natural, just like me!"

It was not long though before he decided to throw her a curve and spun them around.

She let out a yelp, and she tightened her grip on her brother.

Constantin let out a laugh. "Relax, sorellina. I've got you."

When he spun them around again, she caught a glimpse of Agostino, leaning against the doorway, a beaming smile on his face.

Constantin continued the dance for a couple of minutes, reassuring her the couple of times she stumbled, before bringing them to a stop. He enveloped his sister in a big hug. "You were outstanding, sorellina!"

Agostino strolled into the room, clapping as he walked. "*Bravi!*"

She felt her cheeks go slightly pink, just glad she had not made a complete fool of herself.

"*Grazie*, Papà." Constantin replied, giving a large bow.

"You're every bit as gifted, elegant, and graceful as your mother was, *tesorino mio*."

"See, that's where we get it from!" There was a mischievous look on Constantin's face. "Which means we must get our loathing of doing dishes from Papà."

She shared a laugh with her brother, before looking back at Agostino. "She liked to dance as well?"

Agostino nodded. "Dancing, singing, painting. She loved anything that was about creating beauty. Though to her, no work of art could ever compare to any of you."

She felt her heart swell yet again. The emptiness of not being wanted and not being cared about that had been with her since she could remember was becoming so close to being filled. "Maybe one day, I'll be as good as she was."

"In all the ways that matter, you already are, *tesorino mio*."

Before she could become completely overwhelmed, Constantin broke the moment.

"In absolutely shocking news, I'm hungry. I'm going to the kitchen and see what there is."

"I told Giuseppe you were coming by so he should be prepared." Agostino's expression was amused.

Constantin laughed as he strolled out of the room. He shouted over his shoulder. "Anything I should bring you, sorellina?"

"I'm okay, but thank you."

When Constantin had disappeared from view, Agostino held his hand out to her. "May I have this dance?"

She subconsciously started thumbing her mother's wedding ring as small knots formed in her stomach. She was nervous about disappointing him. "Constantin... he made me look a lot better than I actually am."

Agostino did not move his hand. "Please, *tesorino mio.*"

She took a deep breath and put her hand in his.

He led her in the same basic waltz her brother had just taught her. "Your mother, she would tell me how much she was looking forward to watching us do things like this."

She could not meet his eyes, so she looked over to the side. The confession that slipped from her lips could not be held back. "I would dream of doing things like this, when I was a kid."

"*Tesorino mio.*" Agostino stopped their dance and pulled her tight against him. "You don't need to dream anymore. None of us do."

"She's watching us...my mother...she's watching."

"Yes, she is, *tesorino mio.* Your Mamma has been watching over you, all these years. All the years that I couldn't."

She nearly flinched at the hurt in his voice. "Like I said the other day, it wasn't your fault."

"Why haven't you told me about what your life has been like?"

Realization hit her like a ton of bricks. The reason she had given herself was that if she talked about her past, there was a risk that her previous occupation could come up. She realized that was not the exclusive reason though. Without being aware of it, she had been trying to protect him, so he did not feel guiltier than he already did. "It can't be changed so it doesn't matter. What does is what we do from here." She tried to ignore the other meaning of her words and how it applied to her own situation.

"You truly are your mother's daughter."

She really wanted to believe what Agostino had said, but she had her doubts. She was certain her mother would have never considered betraying any of them. Not even for a single second.

It was first when she heard a sound that signaled Constantin's return that she pulled back from Agostino. She gave him a kind smile as she gave her eyes a quick dab.

Constantin had a plate full of biscotti in hand. "I know what you said, sorellina, but you have got to have one of these. Giuseppe just took them out of the oven and they are the best ever."

"Don't you say that about everything you eat, Constantin?"

Agostino gave a hearty laugh at her question.

Constantin shook his head. "I will have you know the only reason I'm even attempting to share these is because that's what one has to do with the favorite."

She opened her mouth to protest but her brother cut her off.

"Trust me, sorellina, none of us are under any disillusion that anyone, other than you, is the favorite."

She could see there was little point in countering his claim, so she took one of the biscotti instead. She did notice that Agostino had not tried to correct Constantin.

Her brother's evaluation of the biscotti was indeed correct. "About these being the best ever, I have to concur with you!"

"I told you so!" When he finished the biscotto, he continued. "Paola's going to be making her ricotta and spinach ravioli for the party. For everyone's sake, please, remember to tell her often that they're the best you've ever had."

Agostino was not quite pleased with his son's tone. The look he gave Constantin was even with the slightest hints of warning. "Your wife is carrying your child. If she wants to hear that a thousand times from each of us, you will make sure it happens."

"You're absolutely right, Papà. I'm sorry."

Agostino nodded, satisfied with Constantin's contriteness. "Because of that, I won't tell her what you said," he said with a smile.

"I've made no such promises," Constantin's sister said with a grin.

Constantin cringed and held the rest of the plate out towards his sister. "The rest of these and all that follow our yours if you promise to never tell her that."

She grinned as she took another biscotto. "I suppose that we could make an arrangement. Until Paola wins me over at least."

Her brother shook his head and set the plate to the side. "You know, sorellina, I think you could do with some more dancing practice. Papà, would you like the honors?"

"Absolutely," Agostino replied, as he held out his hand towards her.

Constantin played a simple melody as Agostino led her in a dance. If things could get better, she could not imagine it.

She wondered just how long the dance could last.

The Solaces

Adriana was waiting by the front door when Ignacio pulled up. He greeted her with a grin. "You ready?"

She enthusiastically nodded as he helped her into the car. He had called her yesterday and invited her to the museum in town and she had happily accepted. They had always given her a sense of serenity which she was greatly craving.

She gave her brother a big smile. "So where do you want to start?"

"That's up to you! I want you to show me all your favorites."

She took a quick glance at the guide and headed for the right, Ignacio by her side.

The first stop was a section with works from the Futurism period. The next, Baroque and Rococo works, the one after that all periods of the Renaissance, then Spatialism, then Gothic and finally ending with Neoclassical works and most especially Macchiaioli.

She was equally animated with each and every painting, going into great detail with each piece. Her brother gave her his full attention, and showed equal enthusiasm.

No matter what section they went to, quick glances and whispered conversations could be found. At one

186

point, she smiled at Ignacio. "Seems like I'm still the talk of the town."

"Your disappearance was one of the biggest mysteries this town has ever known. People are excited to finally have it solved." Her brother leaned close to her. "Though none can even come close to us."

She gave him a warm smile in reply.

While the museum was smaller, it was still hours before they were heading back to his car.

They had been driving for a short while, when Ignacio pulled over to the side of the road, next to a cemetery. He cast a cautious look at his sister. "This is where Mamma is buried and this is when I usually visit. Would you be up for it?"

Adriana took a deep breath, her eyes wandering over the vast cemetery. Visiting her mother's grave had not occurred to her before but, now that the opportunity presented itself, she did not know why she had not thought of it earlier. She felt a sense of shame spread through her. It should have been one of the first things she asked to do but Adriana had been so wrapped up in what was happening to herself, she had not even thought about truly and properly honoring her mother. She knew she needed to make it right. She turned back to her brother and nodded.

He smiled a bit and turned the ignition off. After helping her out, Ignacio kept a grip on her hand, giving it a soft squeeze as he led the way into the cemetery.

As they were walking through, Adriana was extremely surprised and extremely moved to see a picture of the deceased on almost every gravestone they passed. It made her see such a place as honoring lives lived. It somehow made her believe a little more in the spirit carrying on after death.

Everywhere she glanced, she could see fresh flowers and well-tended to grounds. The dead were truly not forgotten here.

The siblings entered a mausoleum near the back of the cemetery. She looked around, seeing dozens of vertical burial niches, on either side of the building. Some were inscribed, while others were not.

While they walked over to the left, Adriana tried to remember what she had learned from the Catholic foster family she had been with a few months. When they reached the grave, both made the sign of the cross, and she only remembered to kiss her hand at the end when her brother did.

She took in the picture of her mother. Rosalia looked absolutely radiant, and she felt a lump form in her throat when she realized the picture was very similar to the one that hung around her neck. The picture that had been chosen so the world could see just who Rosalia was had been taken shortly after the birth of her daughter.

Ignacio wrapped his arm around her shoulders. "She's here, Mamma. Your baby girl is finally home."

She leaned her head on his shoulder, not knowing what to say.

"She's safe now, Mamma." Ignacio continued. "You don't have to worry any more. We're going to take care of her, just like you always wanted."

Guilt rushed through Adriana. She could feel it in every last cell in her body.

"Do you want some time alone with her?" Ignacio questioned.

She nodded, not quite trusting herself to speak.

"I'll wait by the car then," he replied. Ignacio gave her temple a quick kiss, then turned back to the niche and crossed himself once more, then headed outside.

She waited until her brother was a safe distance away, before she began to talk, having managed to somewhat compose herself.

"*Ciao*, Mamma. I hope that it's okay that I call you that." She paused, taking a deep breath as she stared at the photo. "I wish I could have known you. I wish this whole mess had never happened. I wish that you were still here, and that I had been able to grow up with my family."

Tears brimmed on her eyes and she did not bother to hold them back. With a shaking hand, she delicately placed her fingers on her mother's picture. "I don't know what to do, Mamma. I can't do what I first came here to do, not anymore. Even if what the Bureau said about him is true, I don't think I care anymore. I know I should tell him and my brothers the truth, but how can I break their hearts like that?

"And what if they never forgive me for it? The past couple of weeks is everything I've ever dreamt of, I don't know if I can handle losing it."

She swiped a couple of tears away but more kept coming. She fiddled with her mother's ring while she continued. "I would give anything to be able to hug you. It's not fair!" She stopped herself from stomping her foot.

"I wish you could tell me what I should do, Mamma. Do I just run away? Or do I stay, tell the truth, and hope for the best?"

A soft breeze swept through the mausoleum and tickled her cheek.

She nodded a bit, to nothing in particular. "Whatever I do, I'll come back here at least once more. I promise you that." She moved her fingers enough to lay her lips on the picture. She took a deep breath as she stepped back and crossed herself, then headed out to her brother.

She kept her head down while she walked, the tears still streaming down her face. She could not even look up when she reached her brother.

Ignacio did not say anything, but instead, he reached out and tightly wrapped his arms around her.

His sister cried into his shoulder, clinging to him like he was a lifesaver in the middle of a storming sea.

Several minutes passed before either said anything. "I miss her too," Ignacio whispered, his voice cracking with pain.

She took a ragged breath. She felt guilty for being so upset. "I didn't even know her."

"In a way, sorellina, I think that makes it even worse."

"Why did all of this have to happen?" Her voice cracked when she spoke.

"I don't know, sorellina. But having you back... to say it helps is an understatement."

She could feel her heart breaking. "All of you have been so wonderful..."

"It's how it would have been. Nothing more, nothing less."

She felt composed enough to pull back a little and look up at her big brother.

He smiled down at her. "Well, we can see how wonderful you think we are when you try to start dating."

She actually managed to smile and shake her head a bit.

"That is of course if we haven't managed to scare off every guy in a hundred-kilometer radius first!"

"Why not two hundred kilometers, just to be on the safe side?"

"That's a very good idea, sorellina! Thanks for that!"

She rolled her eyes but a smile played on her face.

"In the meantime, let's get some gelato. I know the best place in town."

"Sounds good to me."

He opened the car door for her and a short time later they were driving again. She tried to not let her mind wander too much.

Both had opted for a lemon gelato and as they began to eat, Ignacio posed her a question. "So aside from snakes and doing dishes and waking up early,

192

which you know I wholeheartedly agree with, what else aren't you fond of?"

She stopped just short of saying the first thing that popped into her head, which was "loneliness". She tried to keep her expression light. "Running. I'd much rather bike."

Ignacio grinned. "Yet another thing we have in common! Mamma felt the same way."

"Really?" Her voice was soft.

Her brother nodded. "One thing she would always say to us, though, with regards to running: what matters is that you spend more time running towards things you want, rather than running from things you are afraid of."

She felt herself shudder a bit. It was almost as if her question to her mother earlier had been answered.

Ignacio smiled. "I have a little secret for you. Whenever Papà would take us to a toy store or anything like that, I always insisted that I got an extra one and I would always pick out the softest, squishiest stuffed animal I could find."

"Why did you do that?"

Her brother gave her a meaningful look. "Because when you came home, I wanted you to have something to hold, in case you were scared. I'd sneak it into your room the first chance I got."

She moved closer to her brother and laid her head on his shoulder. "I'm so lucky to have you all."

Ignacio wrapped an arm over her shoulders. "No, sorellina. We're the lucky ones to have you."

When her brother dropped her off, she headed straight to Agostino's office and her heart skipped a beat when he was not in there. It was too early for dinner, but she checked the dining room. That was empty as well. Her breath came quicker and quicker as she hurried for the library, glancing in every room along the way. For a reason she did not know, she needed him.

Agostino was putting a book back on the shelf when he looked over and saw her. "*Tesorino mio …*" was all he managed to get out before she wrapped her arms around him. "Is something wrong?" His voice was laced with concern as he held her close.

Her voice was quiet when she spoke. "We visited Mamma, today." She paused, willing herself to continue. "I'm sorry I didn't think to do it sooner."

"*Tesorino mio,*" Agostino's voice was soft. "There's been so much going on. Your mother would understand that and so do I."

"She deserves better."

"She, and we, do have the best, with you."

"That's not true."

194

"Yes, it is, and don't you ever even imply otherwise."

She desperately wanted to believe him, but demons from her past still whispered in her ear.

"Have you ever wondered why I call you *tesorino mio*?"

"Why?"

"From the moment I saw you, from the moment you took your first breath, I knew that I had the greatest treasure in the world."

She bit back a moan of pain. What she had once been ready to do would have destroyed him. She was not even sure that she deserved forgiveness, even if no damage had been done. Her arms wrapped tighter around him. "Don't let me go."

"Nothing could ever make me do that, *tesorino mio*."

She hoped with every fiber of her being, that that would be the case.

The Apologies

Adriana made her way to Agostino's office. She had told him a couple days ago to continue with the process of hiring her a driver. The interviews had been scheduled for that day.

The only reason she asked him to resume the process was after a conversation they had had. She brought it up because it crossed her mind that it could be seen as odd that she had just brought the whole thing to a halt. She had said, though, that she was not ready to get back to the gallery, and Agostino had pointed out that the driver was for wherever she wished to go for the times he was not at her immediate disposal and not just to and from work.

The files for the three candidates were already on his desk when she walked in.

After a warm greeting that had become the norm for them, any time they were apart for a decent amount of time, he gave her a reassuring look. "Just so you know, Sergio will be stopping by later today. There's an issue I need his help with."

She thought it rather convenient that he would have a computer issue just days before the party but she said nothing about it. She was not sure how she would react to seeing Sergio for the first time after her first morning home, so she tried to not think about it too much and decided to take it as it came.

196

"Shall we review the files, one more time?" When she nodded, he opened the first one.

All three of the candidates were men and all were closer in age to him than to her. Another thing they had in common was they were all rather physical fit. The thought crossed her mind that they could serve a dual purpose; as both a driver and a sort of bodyguard.

During the interviews, it was Agostino who asked all the questions, while she listened. All three made a point of addressing her as much as him, though.

Each one took a good amount of time, as Agostino was very thorough with his questions. It was clear that it was a matter that he took very seriously.

When the last one departed, Agostino turned towards her. "Which one do you think is best?"

"The one who just left. They all seem equally qualified, but there was something about the way the third candidate carried himself that I like."

Agostino nodded. "Agreed. I'll call him shortly and tell him he can start on Monday. The car will first be delivered then, at any rate."

The car Agostino had selected for the one to transport her around was identical to the one he drove himself. She left him to make the call. As she was heading down the hall, Marie was passing her.

Adriana did not know why she was struck by the thought, but there was something she wanted to ask the maid. "Marie?"

The maid quickly turned around. "Yes, Signorina Gismondi?"

"Do you have a minute? There's something I'd like to ask you, please."

"Of course! What is it you would like to know?"

"What was your relationship with my mother like?"

Marie's smile was sad. "Your mother was one of my closest friends. I was hired shortly after Signora Gismondi found out she was pregnant with your eldest brother. Your father would not hear of her doing so much, so I was brought on. After the first week, it was like Signora Gismondi and I had known each other our whole lives."

While she was not surprised that Agostino would make that sort of decision, Adriana did see a contradiction that did not make sense to her. "But you have children of your own. It was hardly fair to make you do the things he did not want my mother to have to do."

Marie lightly laughed. "You misunderstand, Signorina. I was not responsible for all the household things. Signora Gismondi would have never allowed it!

I helped lighten her workload. The times where we both were expecting our little ones; your mother would insist on splitting the duties evenly and she would not hear of anything else. One such instance is the smell of raw meat didn't bother me the way it did her, so I took more of the cooking duties and she saw to other things when she was pregnant with your brothers."

"Forgive my curiosity, but if you two were so close, why do you call her Signora Gismondi?"

Marie's tone was very matter of fact. "She had told me I was welcome to call her by her given name but I made the choice to call her as I do. It was and is the respect she deserves." She paused for a few moments. "It is the same reason I call your father Signore Gismondi."

"Why do you respect him so much?" Wonder was the only thing in her tone.

"All of my children have had dreams. Dreams that could only be achieved through some of the most expensive schools in the country. While my salary has always been very generous, it was not enough to give them what they wanted. I tried to keep it secret but when your father found out, he insisted on paying their way. On top of that, he provided their living expenses, so they only had to focus on their studies. There is no better bonus that I could wish."

The only thing she could do was nod. "*Grazie*, Marie."

The maid gave her quick curtsey and continued on her previous path.

About an hour later, Adriana was headed back down the hall when her eyes landed on the youngest of her older brothers.

"*Ciao,* Sergio." Adriana was nervous.

"*Ciao,*" he replied. "Papà needed my help with a computer thing, but it was quickly solved. I was trying to find you, before I headed out."

She nodded and tried to take a deep breath. "You'll be at the party on Saturday, right?"

"Of course, we will be." His tone lacked enthusiasm.

The words tumbled out before she could stop them. "Why do you hate me so much?"

"I don't … hate you."

"Then what do you feel? Please, Sergio, I want to understand."

Her words finally cracked his reserved exterior. "For me, you were always something so abstract. I only knew what you looked like through a picture. I didn't have any of my own memories of you. I only had what others told me.

"Because of how close we are in age, with every accomplishment and every milestone I had, they would all inevitably be wondering what was happening with you. I was scared on my first day of school, they would talk about how you might potentially handle it. I got top grades, they'd wonder what subjects you liked and didn't like. I got married and they'd speculate if you had found the right one yet or not."

She held her tongue, because it seemed like he was not yet done.

"It drove me mad. I felt like if I tried to tell them to stop, they would only get angry with me. So, I gritted my teeth and endured it. After a while, it was just easier to turn my aggravation towards you, somebody that I really had no idea about, rather than people I saw every single day.

"Sometimes, I never knew my place in the family. I was the youngest but I wasn't. I would be the last to do things but maybe I wouldn't. I did everything right but I didn't. I was in constant competition, willing and unwilling, with a ghost and there was no way I could possibly win.

"When Papà told us about you … I figured I'd get more pushed to the side than ever, and as a matter of fact … you're the first one, aside from my wife, to actually ask me how I feel about the whole thing. When it seemed like my fear was becoming a reality … I just cracked."

She reached out and clasped onto his hand. The feelings of misplacement from her childhood had only first began to fade in the past few weeks, so she was way too familiar with the raw ache. His sister realized that in a bizarre way, she was best to understand Sergio, even if she knew him the least. "I'm truly sorry that you've had to go through all that."

Sergio finally broke down, quietly at first, then more and more with each passing second.

She hated seeing him like that, so she did the only thing she could think of, and pulled her brother in for a tight hug. "You're not going to get pushed out and forgotten. I swear it. I won't let it happen. I won't have you feel what I have almost all my life."

Her brother clung to her, years of tears streaming down his face and onto her shoulder.

"It's going to be better from now on. I promise." She whispered the reassurance several times over.

When Sergio finally pulled back, she kept her hands on his arms.

"I'm sorry." His voice was soft. "For everything."

"Let's forget about it. Let's make this our fresh start."

Her brother nodded. "I do really have to go now. I'll see you soon though … sorellina."

There was a beaming smile on her face as she waved goodbye. She was not worried. It would take a little more time, but she knew they were on their way to having a close relationship.

When she heard the door shut, she made quick strides for Agostino's office. She did not even bother pausing to see if he was in the middle of something. "We need to talk about Sergio."

"What has he done now?"

"That's just it! He hasn't done anything. It's what hasn't been done for him that's the problem!"

"What are you talking about?"

"He's felt like he's been completely overlooked in this whole situation."

Agostino's expression held hints of annoyance. "His sister has finally come home, safe and sound. He should be nothing but relieved and happy!"

"He feels what he feels. We don't have to agree with it, but we have to understand it! He shouldn't feel like he's not a whole part of this family."

"He knows he's a part of this family."

Her voice was low and shaky. "Knowing and feeling are two entirely different things."

Something about her tone struck Agostino, and he quickly pulled her into his arms. "You're right, *tesorino mio*. You're absolutely right. I'm sorry."

She leaned on him as she fought the bad memories that still lurked on the edges of her mind. "Talk to Sergio. Even better, listen to him. Let him say his piece and don't criticize him for it. Get the rest of the family to do the same. Please, do it for him."

"I'll do it for all of us."

"Do it as soon as you can. It'll mean the world to him."

"The first chance I get, I will call him."

She gave him a peck on the cheek as she pulled back and gave him a grateful smile.

Near the stairs, a picture of her mother hung. She stopped in front of it and touched it with her right hand while the fingers of her left curled around her locket. "I hope I handled that as well as you would have, Mamma."

Looking like her mother was one thing. What mattered to her more was being the kind of person her mother had been.

She hoped with all her heart that she would get the chance.

The Songs

Adriana rummaged through the vast array of cabinets in the kitchen. She was trying to assemble all the remaining ingredients that were needed for her mother's special blackberry pie. Agostino had shown her the recipe the night before. He had told her that they would be responsible for the dessert and she had asked what her mother's favorite thing to make was.

They had started the process the night before, mixing the blackberries with brown sugar and lemon zest and leaving them to sit until the next morning. Agostino had told her that her mother had always insisted that letting it sit overnight was the only acceptable way to do it.

She was putting the last of the ingredients for the crust on the counter when Agostino walked into the kitchen, his laptop in hand. When she gave him a quizzical look, he smiled. "We're going to be making you mother's special pie, so I thought it fitting for us to listen to her, while we work."

Her breath caught in her throat. It was indeed a brilliant idea and Adriana was struck with the realization why she had not asked before. Seeing pictures of her mother and hearing stories about her was one thing, but she felt that all the conflict, all the guilt, all the shame and all the fear that she had been battling lately would suddenly become that much more real if she had something so tangible of her mother's.

Despite her anxiety, she was now desperate to experience the one part of her mother that was not robbed from her. She steeled herself and nodded her head.

Agostino cued up the music and stepped back from the computer.

She closed her eyes, as the sound of her mother's voice filled the kitchen. There were no filters, no instruments to distract, just a pure and angelic voice permeating her ears. She wondered what it would be like to hear that voice, when she was sick, or when she was scared, or when she was upset. She was pretty sure it would be like a magic wand, something to make everything better right away, because that's what it was doing for her in that exact moment. Her breath was ragged and despite her efforts, she felt the tears glide down her cheeks.

The next thing she knew, Agostino had folded his arms around her, holding her tight.

Her arms automatically curled around him, and despite her upset state, felt a sense of comfort she had always assumed would be denied to her. "Mamma's voice…. it's… amazing." Her own voice was no louder than a whisper.

"She loved you every bit as much as I do, *tesorino mio.*"

Adriana did not feel like she had any right to ask for what she was about to, but she could not help herself. "Say it again."

"I love you. Every single second of every single day. I always have, and I always will. I was only waiting for you to be ready to hear it."

She sighed as she felt her heart simultaneously heal and break. Imaginings of him holding her and of her mother singing to her through various stages of her life flashed through her mind, and she felt utterly robbed of what could have been.

Even when she had composed herself again, she remained where she was for a little while longer.

When she eventually pulled back, she smiled up at Agostino. "We'd better get to work. Five pies aren't going to make themselves."

"As you wish, *tesorino mio*." He quickly kissed her forehead before letting her go.

The ingredients were mixed and they set the five pieces of dough in the fridge. Having a half-hour to wait, Agostino gathered the dirty dishes and she quickly followed suit.

"It is a good thing that you don't hate drying as much as you hate washing." His expression was amused as he held a tea towel out to her.

It had become their system on the weekends, when Giuseppe and Marie had free, for the items that could not be placed in the dishwasher. She knew he was about as fond of washing as she was and had said they could take turns, but he would not hear of it. A smile was on her face as she took the towel.

A sentimental look crossed his face. "You smiled at me, for the first time, right over there." He pointed to where a chair stood by the small table. "I had you in your car seat, while I was preparing dinner. I came over to check on you and you looked right at me and smiled. It was one day before you turned a month old."

She looked at him in wonder. "How could you possibly remember that?"

"You have one of the most beautiful smiles I have ever seen. There is no way I could ever forget the first time I saw it."

She looked down, trying to focus on the bowl she was drying, so she did not become completely overwhelmed.

"It wasn't the only developmental milestone I got to see with you. I got to hear your laugh, once, before you were taken." Agostino looked over to the side.

Memories from her first dinner back home sprang in her mind. She remembered thinking his reaction when Valentino was telling the skiing disaster story had nothing to do with her, but she realized she was completely and utterly wrong. It had had everything to do with her. She stopped him from taking another dish up and turned Agostino to face her. "We all missed out on so much but we don't have to anymore. That's what we need to think about now."

"You are absolutely right, *tesorino mio.*"

Shortly after the dishes were done, it was time to roll out the dough and assemble the pies. She wished she had learned the trick about wrapping the dough around the rolling pin a lot sooner. It would have most likely saved her from buying so many pre-made crusts.

They had just finished setting the pies in the large oven, when there was a light knock on the kitchen door, and she looked over in surprise before turning her gaze towards Agostino. None of her brothers had mentioned that they would be coming by.

"I'm sorry, *tesorino mio.* I forgot to mention a dear friend of mine was going to be briefly visiting today."

"It's fine."

Agostino nodded and turned back towards the door. "Come in!"

A man of an age with Agostino entered the kitchen. He had wiry, salt and pepper hair and he was dressed in black slacks, a black shirt, and a white clerical collar.

"Gio!" Agostino gave the newcomer a warm smile and embrace.

The man returned the greeting in kind. "It's good to see you, 'Tino."

Agostino turned towards her. "*Tesorino mio,* allow me to introduce you to one of my closest friends, Father Gioachino Vozzella. Gio, my daughter."

She held her hand out to him and he tightly clasped it in both of his. The pictures Macario had shown her stirred in her mind, and she connected the face and the name and realized he was the man who had baptized her.

His eyes were swimming with a mixture of relief and endearment and something else she could not quite place. "Welcome home," Father Vozzella's voice was soft.

"*Grazie.*" Her own voice was no louder than his.

"I know you can't stay for long, Gio, but would you care for some coffee?"

"Yes, please."

While Agostino got to work, she gave the priest a small smile. The thought of two people such as Agostino and Father Vozzella being such good friends did not strike her as bizarre, as it would have once done. "May I ask how long you two have known each other?"

Father Vozzella smiled warmly, and there were hints of pride. "I've known your father for over half a century. We've been friends since our first day in primary school. I presided over your parent's wedding and I have baptized every one of you."

Father Vozzella had had a couple of sips of coffee when Agostino's phone rang. He gave it a quick glance. "Could you two excuse me for a minute, please? It's Paola, and I want to make sure she isn't stressing herself out over anything to do with the party."

When both nodded, he quickly took his phone up and headed out of the kitchen.

She really had no idea what to say to the priest but was saved when Father Vozzella spoke first.

"Your father ... it's been years since I've seen him like this."

His expression made the words tumble out of her mouth before she could even think about stopping them. If there was a person that could give her the answers she sought, she had a feeling it was the priest. "Can everything really be forgiven? Even the breaking of one of the commandments? Like the one about the parents?" She could feel the warmth spreading on her cheeks.

Father Vozzella gave her a kind look. "No one should feel shame, in not knowing something they were not given an opportunity to learn." After giving her shoulder a reassuring squeeze, he continued. "Honor thy father and thy mother, I believe, is what you are referring to. And to answer your question, yes, that is forgivable."

"How can you be so sure?"

"I have to believe it." After a long pause, he continued. "One of the seven, sacred sacraments in the Church is the Sacrament of Penance. It is where a person confesses the mortal sins they have committed, in hopes to obtain absolution. During the sacrament, a priest, such as myself, is a minister of Christ's mercy. That is to say, it is not me who forgives the sins, but Christ himself. Every act of Penance I administer, I'm bound by the seal of confession. Succinctly said, I am not to reveal anything, anyone tells me during their confession. There are few exceptions to this seal. There are some sins considered too grave, that it is not within my power to give absolution for. Some matters, only a bishop or the Holy See can grant that. I have had one such instance in my entire time in the Church."

Her eyes were locked with his, as she felt her heart begin to race.

Father Vozzella took a deep breath and continued. "Now, there are, for lack of a better phrase, some grey areas about me passing on information I have heard during a confession, so long as I do not reveal the identity of the person. I had to make such a decision mere weeks ago."

212

It finally clicked in her head that Father Vozzella was the person Macario had referred to, the one Agostino trusted implicitly. He was the reason her family found out about her and reached out to her. "Why did you do it?" Her tone was a mix of wonder and amazement.

"I would rather risk an eternity in Hell, than let one of the people dearest to me continue living in it."

As tempted as she was to try to get more information from him, she knew he had put himself in a precarious enough position, and she could not, with good conscious, ask him for anymore. He was ultimately the reason she had found her way home. Instead, she threw her arms around the priest as grateful tears sprung in her yes. "Thank you is nowhere close to what you are owed."

"I am not owed anything."

It was a while before she pulled back, her face swimming with gratitude. There was nervousness there as well, though, as there was something she needed to ask him. She hoped he would give her the answer she was hoping for. "Can he really forgive anything?"

Father Vozzella clasped her face and his gaze was gentle. "For you, of course he can."

She desperately wanted to believe him, but she could not help but still have doubts.

He glanced at his watch. "I'm very sorry, but I must take my leave now. I'll try to find your father on my way out but if I don't, could you please tell him I say goodbye?" He paused briefly before he reached out and put a hand on her arm. "If there is ever anything you need, just say and I'll be here for you."

Her tumultuous emotions made it hard for her to speak so she merely nodded.

Father Vozzella seemed to understand, as he simply smiled in reply.

A brief time after the priest made his exit, Agostino came back into the kitchen. "I saw Gio on his way out so you don't need to tell me goodbye from him."

"He told me ... what he did."

Agostino nodded. "You can understand, though, why I thought it was his place to tell you that he was the one who came to me, and the circumstances in which he found out?"

"I know he said he couldn't reveal who told him about me, but do you have any idea whom it could have been? I don't want to get him in even the slightest trouble ... but I just ... want to know the how."

He contemplated her request for a few moments. "I just want to be clear that he never, ever gave me a name. It was something I was able to figure out on my

214

own, based on when he came to me. The person who gave him the information was the woman who had been your nanny. Gio's exact words to me were: there is a young woman in town with the same birthmark as your daughter. Here is where she can be found."

Part of her was confused. While she was unsure about what exactly a mortal sin was, she was at least sure that it was something pretty severe, especially given Father Vozzella all but saying it was the only case he had had, where he had needed to go to his superiors. She could not see how being knocked unconscious could equate to needing absolution. Perhaps her nanny had always had a sense of guilt over what happened.

Another part of her was wracking her brain to try to remember any such encounter. The only time she could recall being careless about her birthmark, was her first time in the library. The fact that she must have slipped at another point, when the woman who could recognize it was around, and set everything in motion, solidified her belief that her reunion with her family was meant to happen.

"Thank you for telling me."

"You're welcome, *tesorino mio*."

The timer for the oven sounded and they set the pies on the counter to cool.

Agostino gave her a praising smile. "They look and smell just as good as your mother's."

"I couldn't have done it without your help."

"That is something that you will always have."

"I know."

"It'll be a while before they're completely cooled. We can go into town and pick up the remaining items for tomorrow, in the meantime."

Agostino drove cautiously as he had always done. She did wonder if he always drove in such a manner, or if it had something to do with her being in the car. His voice interrupted her thoughts.

"I must ask, is this how your brothers' have driven?"

She wracked her brain, trying to come up with a diplomatic answer.

The lack of a prompt reply from her spoke volumes to Agostino. "That tells me all I need to know." He did not look particularly pleased.

"I'm sure they didn't do anything, they didn't feel confident about." She was doing her best, to come to her brothers' defense.

"Confidence and safety are not one in the same." Agostino seemed to realize the extra bite in his tone and pulled into a small parking lot outside of a shop on the side of the road and parked the car. He turned towards her. "It's not you that I'm upset with."

"Maybe by their standards, they were being cautious. Sometimes, things can look and seem very different in the passenger seat." She remembered she was not supposed to know how to drive. "So, I've heard."

"While your attempt to protect your brothers is admirable, I still intend to have a talk with each and every one of them."

"Please, I don't want to make a big deal out of this. I'm probably just overreacting."

Agostino held her gaze for several long moments. "That 'probably' is what tells me with certainty that you are not overreacting. There shouldn't have been a single moment that you felt unsure. All it takes is one split second, and there could have been an accident, and you could have been hurt, or…" He turned his head away, the worst-case scenario clearly flashing through his mind.

As soon as she freed herself from the seat belt, she wrapped her arms around Agostino's shoulders, her forehead resting against his neck. "Please, don't think about that."

His cheek pressed against the top of her head as his arms drew her closer. "I try not to, *tesorino mio*. Believe me, I do. But sometimes…"

Her arms tightened around him. "Then come and talk to me. Promise me you'll do that."

"It's me, who is supposed to be taking care of you, not the other way around."

"We take care of each other."

When they reached the market, she pulled out the list, checking off each item as they put it in the basket.

It took them a little longer than it likely would have, had she been by herself, as Agostino was extremely discerning about the produce.

As they worked their way through the store, employees and fellow customers greeted them with smiles and nods, which they both returned.

They were nearly done when a man approached them. By his nametag, she could see that he was the manager.

He greeted the both of them, before turning his attention to Agostino. "Signore Gismondi, I'm terribly sorry to interrupt, but do you have a minute? There's something I need to discuss with you."

She knew Agostino's company had a lot of subsidiaries and assumed this store must be one of

218

them. Agostino looked like he was about to object. She reasoned that it was because he was always very careful to not split his attention between her and work when they were together, and decided to intervene. "It's fine. I wanted to go outside for a few minutes anyways."

"I promise I won't be long."

She gave him a smile on her way out.

She was down to the last couple of drags on her cigarette, when she noticed a man approaching, his eyes fixed on her. She averted her gaze but tried to watch him out of the corner of her eye. Her body tensed as he stopped right in front of her.

"Well, you're the prettiest little thing I've seen in a long time."

She took a couple of steps to the side, trying to distance herself from the man.

This just made him move closer to her. "Why so shy? I'm only trying to tell you how beautiful you are."

Before she could even speak, the man had grabbed onto her wrist and tried yanking her to him.

"Let me go!" She surprised herself with her tone. It was much more of a command than a scared request. She tried yanking her hand away but his grip was tight.

It was only a moment later that she felt him slip her free. She started automatically rubbing her wrist and when she finally looked up, her eyes widened.

There was a fire in Agostino's eyes but his face was as hard and cold as marble. One hand was curled around the man's collar, and the other had his wrist in a vice like pinch. He had placed himself squarely between his daughter and the man. "Do you have any idea of what you've just done?" Agostino's voice was low, which made it all that more terrifying.

The man paled considerably and it was several attempts before words came out. "Sig… Sig… Signore Gismondi! I… I had no idea! If I had known… I would have never… I'm truly sorry!"

She was sorely tempted to just step back and watch what happened. Perhaps the man would quicker learn not to take liberties with whatever woman he pleased. She looked closer at Agostino and realized there was much more to his reaction than just a 'men aren't allowed near my daughter' attitude. It was something much deeper than that, and she realized it was fear. What must it have been like for him just now, mere weeks after getting her back, to come out and see what must have looked like someone trying to haul her off? She could not stand by and let him suffer those thoughts, just to teach some idiot a lesson.

When she saw him slowly start to apply more pressure to the man's wrist, her hand reached out and stilled Agostino with a gentle touch. "I just want him away from me. Please."

"You are never to come anywhere near my daughter again. Do you understand?" What would happen to the man if he did, did not need to be said.

The man nodded, shooting a fearful look at her. The second he was released from Agostino's grip, he rushed for his car as quickly as possible. He barely shut the door before he tore across the parking lot.

Agostino stared after him, until the man disappeared from view, then he turned his full attention on her. "Are you hurt?"

"I'm fine," she lied a bit. Her wrist had a dull ache, but she did not want him thinking about that. "You came just in time."

"No one is to treat you like that. If anything like that should ever happen again, you come to me immediately."

She nodded. "I will. I promise." Her arms wrapped around Agostino. "I know you'll keep me safe."

He returned her embrace. "Yes, I will, *tesorino mio*. Yes, I will."

When the day had reached its end, she prepared for bed. The ups and the downs from the day had made her feel exhausted, but she was having a bit of trouble falling asleep. The things she had discovered, the events that had happened and speculation of what the next day would bring whirled around in her mind. When she looked over at her bedside table, she knew what she needed to help lull her to sleep.

She opened the music box from Agostino and drifted off, while the music played.

The Moments

Adriana gazed into the mirror, making sure everything was just right. She had chosen a cream, silk dress and a pair of pale pumps, with a clear heel. Her hair was piled on her head and she had cinched a short midnight blue scarf around her neck. The locket from Valentino hung around her neck, and the bracelet from Constantin adorned her wrist. Her mother's wedding ring was on her finger, as it always was, and on her ears were a pair of emerald and diamond earrings Agostino had given her the other day, just because.

She could not remember why she had detested her morning routine in the beginning. It was now a calming process to start the day, something that gave her a sense of serenity, even if she did not know exactly why.

One last check and she made her way to the sitting room. She was not surprised to find Agostino already waiting there.

He turned around when he heard her entrance and a beaming smile broke on his face. "*Tesorino mio*, you look exquisite."

"*Grazie*." There was a pleased smile on her face. It failed, however, to completely mask the nerves she had been battling with all morning.

Agostino cupped her face with both of his hands. "Everyone already loves you. You have nothing to be worried about."

She let his words echo in her head while they waited for everyone to arrive.

The clock was just striking the hour, when they heard a commotion that got louder with each passing second.

She barely had time to register what was happening when she heard shouting. *"Zia! Zia! Zia!"* A small blur with dark hair barreled towards her.

She was almost knocked off her feet when the little blur finally came into contact with her. The lower part of herself was encased in a vice like grip and she tried to orientate herself.

"Oh *Zia*, I kept telling Papà that he needed to bring me to you right away but he wouldn't listen!" The little girl spoke so quickly, Adriana was almost struggling to keep up. "We are going to have so much fun! I've brought my coloring things, and my hair things, my dolls and I've planned so many games for us to play!"

A brunette woman with a bob cut made her way over to them. "Francesca! What have we talked about? You need to take a breath in between each thought!"

Francesca rolled her eyes and shook her head.

The woman stretched her arms out and kissed her on both cheeks. "I'm Ciana, Macario's wife. It's so nice to finally meet you!"

She smiled sweetly. "It's so nice to finally meet you too! If my brother forgot to say it, thank you for the new face wash!"

Ciana held her gaze for a couple of moments, and then turned towards her husband. "Macario!"

He jumped slightly as he turned his head towards his wife. "Yes, *amore mio*?"

"You forgot to tell her why I said to throw the face wash out, didn't you?"

Macario looked guilty. "Maybe. *Amore*, you know I love hearing about your work, but sometimes there are just so many big words..."

Ciana rolled her eyes. "Big words? You're a lawyer, Macario!" He was trying to muster something to say in his defense, when she shook her head. "You're so lucky I love you so much!"

"Yes, *amore*!" He replied automatically.

Ciana turned her attention back to her sister-in-law. "What my lovely husband forgot to tell you is the brand I said to throw out, sneaks in extra mineral oil into the product, and it is horrible for the skin!"

"How do you know that?"

Ciana smiled. "I came up with the original formula. When they corrupted it, I quit!"

Francesca stomped her foot. "Okay, can I now play with my *zia*?"

Ciana looked down at her daughter. "Have you even asked her if she wants to play with you?"

"Of course, she does, Mamma! Why would I need to ask?"

She bit down on a laugh and squatted down, so she was eye level with Francesca. "There's a lot of people I need to say hi to. Like your brothers and father, for starters. And all the rest of your aunts and uncles and cousins when they get here. When I'm done with all that, then we can play."

Francesca sighed. "Okay, fine! Just don't take too long!"

As she straightened up, she was greeted by the sight of the younger Agostino, known in the family as Tino.

Macario's oldest son was a very serious, budding young man. Anyone who knew her brother on a superficial level would probably wonder how they could possibly be father and son, but she had seen past Macario's mask enough to know that Tino was just like his father.

"*Ciao, Zia.*" He warmly embraced her.

Tommaso was the next to greet her. He was nearly a carbon copy of his mother, but he had Macario's smile.

"My turn now," her brother said as he wrapped his arms around her.

Francesca stomped her foot. "You've had weeks. Weeks! With her. I've had five minutes!"

When Macario pulled back, his expression clearly said he was bracing to hear about that for a long time.

His sister tried to give him a reassuring smile, though the second there was enough distance between the two of them, Francesca gripped onto her aunt's leg.

The next to arrive were Constantin and Paola. Giovanni and Lorenzo were right behind them, while Paola had Nicolo by the hand. One would probably not guess that Paola was pregnant, if not for the slight bump protruding from her stomach.

The boys' greeting was quick as they hurried off with Francesca, who was greatly relieved to have someone to play with. It gave her a chance to properly meet her sister-in-law.

Paola had auburn hair and green eyes and, either she was exactly like her husband and had an incredible amount of energy, or she had become an expert in masking just how tired she actually was.

She gave Paola an apologetic look. "Could you remind me when the due date is again?"

Paola turned her head to her husband, her expression incredulous. "You seriously haven't told her? You even said it was a sign that we were going to get her back! Not to mention it's the only one of my due dates you've actually been able to remember!" She shook her head in disbelief, ignoring when Constantin opened his mouth and turned back to her sister-in-law. "Four months from now. The same day as your birthday, actually." Paola's voice was soft.

She felt her heart skip a beat. A baby actually being born on their due date was far from the norm, but she found herself hoping that would be the case. It would be extremely poetic if she shared a birthday with the first niece or nephew who was born after she came home. When she reached out and squeezed Paola's hands, she could tell her sister-in-law shared the same sentiment.

"I'm just hoping he's finally given me a girl this time!"

"Every time you make it seem like it's my fault."

"Do I have to get Dante to explain it to you, again?"

"It's not like it's a conscious decision on my part."

228

His wife narrowed her eyes at Constantin. "I still have my suspicions."

"Hey, it took Mamma seven tries, before she got her girl."

The look Paola gave him made it clear that was not an idea she would like to entertain. "I'm home with the boys all day, so anytime you want to visit, feel free to! I love my sons but I miss talking with other grown-ups."

"What do you mean?" Constantin questioned. "You have me to talk to every night!"

Paola regarded her husband for a few seconds before turning her attention back to her sister-in-law. "He obviously missed the part where I said grown-ups."

This time, she did not bother trying to hide her laugh.

Constantin grimaced. "You two are going to be teaming up against me all the time, aren't you?"

"Most likely, yes." There was no hesitation in Paola's reply.

While Constantin sought out his older brother for solace, Valentino and his family arrived.

Valentino's wife, Esta, was almost the polar opposite of him, both physically and personality wise.

One look though was all it took to know they were perfect for each other.

Elena was the first forward, followed by her little sister, Viviana and her little brother Enzo.

Out of the corner of her eye, she saw her eldest niece frantically typing on her smartphone.

"I'll be taking that now." Valentino plucked the phone out of her hand. "You can have it back on the way home."

"I was just sending one quick message!" Elena moaned.

"Then it won't be a problem if it's in my pocket for the rest of the day!"

"*Nonno.*" Elena gave Agostino a pleading look.

"Your father is right."

Elena sighed in defeat and sulked off towards her cousins.

She was just pulling back from Esta when she heard the snap of her brother's camera. He had decided that the proper camera was in order that day. Her hunch was there would be several albums full of pictures from that day if Valentino had his way. She found herself looking forward to seeing each and every one.

Esta kept her hands on her sister-in-law's arms. "You like flowers, right?" When she nodded, Esta continued. "You're welcome to pop by the shop any time. I've heard that you have an excellent eye and I'd love your opinion on some of the arrangements I've been pondering."

Her cheeks became warm as she smiled at Esta. She was absolutely flattered, and she was certain Esta meant what she had said.

Sergio and Gina came in, Vincenzo snuggly on his mother's hip.

She had been most nervous about meeting Gina, given that her and Sergio's reconciliation was still rather fresh. If Gina held even a slight grudge against her, she could not detect it.

"You'll have to excuse me for a moment," Gina said with amusement. "Paola won't forgive me if I don't get Vincenzo over to her as soon as possible. She loves holding babies she can just give back."

Her voice was soft when she spoke to her brother. "I'm really glad you're here."

"Likewise." Sergio's voice was as soft as hers.

She blinked the happy tears back as she held her brother tight. She had made a point of calling all their brothers the night before and making them promise they would make a point of making Sergio feel included. There was no doubt in her mind that they would keep that promise.

Ignacio and Bellissa and Dante and Natala and all the kids arrived at the same time.

New leg attachments were made when Ignacio's identical twin daughters, Cosetta and Lauretta, decided they needed to be as close as humanly possible to their aunt.

While Ignacio hugged her, he took the opportunity to whisper in his sister's ear. "Cosetta has the pink ribbon in her hair and Lauretta the yellow."

She was eternally grateful for that bit of information. While it was something that was probably done for the benefit of the whole family, she would have felt guilty calling one of them by the wrong name.

Matteo and Elisa were like night and day. Where Elisa was cautious, Matteo was reckless. When Elisa clung to her mother, Matteo was blazing around the room. What Matteo found fascinating, Elisa found scary.

She gave her niece a soft smile as she bent down to her height. "All of this is a lot for me too."

Elisa threw her arms around her aunt's neck and held tight, with no regards for her cousins who still clung to the lower limbs of their aunt.

She held Elisa equally as tight, if not the slightest bit more. These moments were something that could never be taken from her. Her memory would forever be burned with them.

Natala's temperament was nearly identical to her husband's. Infinite patience, infinite empathy and infinite understanding. She gave her sister-in-law a kind smile. "Whenever you need something ... just let me know. My schedule revolves around the school schedule ... but if needed ... I'm here for you."

She could only think of her sister-in-law as an amazing teacher and an amazing person. It crossed her mind that Natala and her brother most likely never actually fought, but instead seriously debated a matter. Stable families surrounded her, and she could not be more grateful. She battled against the tears that welled in her eyes.

It was only when Francesca stomped over to her that she was snapped out of her thoughts.

"That's everybody! Now, we play!" Francesca already had a hand full of cards.

She shook her head and laughed, as she realized her niece would always get her way. She only half-listened as Francesca explained the spontaneous, yet very complicated, rules of her game. A glance around at the more than two dozen people had her heart swell.

She felt whole for the first time in her life.

The Connections

Her niece finally calmed down from winning and gave her a huge hug. "We can do this every week, right, *zia*?"

Francesca's aunt realized she could not play the avoidance game any longer. As afraid of the consequences as she was, she finally realized there were more than two dozen peoples' interests at play. She had to give them fair warning, so they could protect themselves if need be. It could no longer just be about her. She blinked quickly, to hide the tears. "I certainly hope so. Though there is something I need you to do for me right now. I need you to find your papà and bring him over to me."

"Okay!" Francesca hurried off. It took her mere seconds to spot her father, and she near literally pulled him over.

"I need to talk with you right now." His sister's eyes were pleading.

Macario nodded and squatted down to Francesca. "*Cucciola*, why don't we play hide and seek? You go over there and count to one hundred, while your *zia* and I hide. If anyone asks where we are, you just tell them we're playing a game."

"Okay!" Francesca ran over to the corner and started counting.

Her brother grabbed onto her hand and snuck her out of the sitting room. "This way…" he said softly and Macario led her to the library. "What is it, sorellina?"

Her mouth opened and closed. She paced back and forth, hugging herself. "There's something I need to tell you. You have to promise you won't hate me for it!"

"You know I could never hate you, sorellina!"

"You have to realize that things aren't the same as they were before. If I could have done it differently…"

Macario's smile was amused, as he stepped in front of his sister to stop her from pacing. "Is this the part where you tell me when you first came here, you were on assignment from the FBI?"

She froze in place. "You knew that?!"

He nodded. "Before you even stepped off the plane, we knew. It's why we steered clear of the general area you were in, at first. Thank goodness the information about you being our sister came from Father Vozzella or we may have never found out. But when we definitively found out the truth, we believed enough, that you would realize the choice you should make."

Despite herself, Adriana felt a knot form in her stomach. "If you knew… all the attention… all the kindness…" She could not bring herself to finish her thought.

Macario clasped her face and looked her directly in the eyes. "That was us. There was no ulterior motive. We were only trying to show you what life would be like with us."

She did not even bother trying to hide the relief when she sighed. "I believe you."

"What have they said about Papà?"

"They say he's ordered some horrible things! Some brutal killings…"

"What names did they give you?"

"Tito Cavello, Fiorello Ongaro and Enrico Locatelli."

"Tito Cavallo? Did they happen to mention what Cavello had done?" When she shook her head, Macario continued. "He raped six children. The bastard was sick enough to record it. The case should have been a sure thing. He walked on a technicality.

"Fiorello Ongaro? Human trafficker, more specifically early teenage girls. He'd get them addicted to drugs, then force them to work in the sex trade.

"Enrico Locatelli? He tortured his own kid and brutally beat her to death."

"They had it coming." Her voice was soft but resolute.

Macario nodded, and took a deep breath before he continued. "The men who took you, are unsavory, to put it mildly. The quickest way to get to unsavory people, is to make connections with unsavory people. That's what Papà did, because he did not want to leave a single stone unturned when it came to you. The justice he got to dole out along the way was a slight bonus. Each hit he ordered, felt like a blow against those who stole you from us."

She did not give a damn if it was wrong or right, but she felt her heart soar at his words. Her family was willing to move heaven and earth for her, damned the consequences. She felt like her scarf was strangling her, so she ripped it off and threw it to the side, with no idea nor care where it landed. "What do I do now?"

Macario sat down on the edge of the desk. "First, is there any sort of extraction plan for you?"

She shook her head. "No, I've been on my own. Sink or swim, so to say. It's been a black ops operation, so there's no record of it."

"How do you communicate with them?"

"Check-ins once a month. I'd go to one of the bigger cities; Venice, Milan, or Florence, buy a prepaid cell phone, and make the call. 'I have an extra ticket to the opera, if you want to go' was the code phrase for me still being on the case. I'd then break the SIM card, and throw the phone out in a different trash can, after clearing the call log. The next call should be made in two days' time."

"The check-ins also let them know to keep financing the gallery, right?"

She nodded in response.

"How many people know of your work here?"

"Two. Grant Marks and Jacob Wentworth. Wentworth at least knows that I was working some angle for Marks, though I don't know if he knows the details."

Macario got lost in thought for a few moments, fermenting a plan. "Okay, here's what we do. For starters, we need to have you officially reclaim your identity as Lucia Gismondi. It'll be a very tedious process but lucky for you, you just happen to have the best lawyer in Italy, who is owed a lot of favors. I should be able to get it pushed through rather quickly.

"The next thing is, you do not check in next time. That should stop the financing of the gallery, cutting that lead."

Despite that she had known that had to be the case, she could not help but let her face fall a little at the reality of it. When she had first started it, even though it was supposed to be nothing more than a cover, she had actually enjoyed it quite a bit.

238

"We'll help you open a new one, don't worry about that. We might have to wait a year or so, just to be safe. Besides, it'll be easier to pass off with the locals. You took some time off to be with us and now you're ready for a new start with a new gallery.

"The last thing is Wentworth and Marks." He took a deep breath. "We found out something about Marks that we'll all talk about later." He held up a hand when she started to question him anyways. "It's best if we all talk about it together. With regards to Wentworth, I can tell you with certainty that he knows exactly what your assignment was. He's the one who gave us the heads up via a couple of middle contacts. We'll just give him a message that the situation has been neutralized and he shouldn't worry about it anymore. We'll talk with Papà and see if he thinks bumping up Wentworth's monthly stipend is a sagacious idea. On the off chance that he does hear about you and puts two and two together and seems like he might be a threat- we'll handle it. Don't worry about that."

She finally felt the weight that had been bearing down on her shoulders disappear, as she realized she was finally out and clear. The next thing she did was to throw her arms around Macario. "You are the best big brother!" She squeezed him tight.

"There's nothing in the world I wouldn't do for you, sorellina." His hug was almost as fierce as her own.

The door flew open at that moment. "Found you!" Francesca exclaimed with glee.

The two adults laughed. "Shall we go tell the others, sorellina?"

She nodded and the trio returned to the sitting room.

When they reached it, her eyes met those of the Gismondi patriarch. Before she could think, she was rushing over to him. "I'm sorry, Papà! I'm so, so sorry!" She threw her arms around his torso, and buried her face in his chest. "I'm sorry, Papà!"

"You have nothing to be sorry for, *tesorino mio*. I never had any doubt that you would never betray us." There was a triumphant look on his face, as he rested his head on top of hers.

The children were sent out for some fresh air. A few were reluctant but were eventually bribed with biscotti. Fortunately, Vincenzo and Nicolo had decided then was an excellent time to take a nap. They had been laid in a room nearby.

Macario filled in the rest of the family. Her father held her the whole time, his fingers gently stroking her birthmark.

Bellissa spoke first. "The clients you had? Were they all art dealers?"

"I believe so. To be honest, there weren't so many. I'm pretty sure you sold more in the time you covered for me." She was embarrassed to admit it.

Bellissa wove that off with a wave of her hand. "Newcomer caution. It just comes with the trade. Not to mention the next time you open a gallery, it'll be as Signorina Gismondi and not some outsider who's trying to live out some silly romantic comedy. I'll go back once more early tomorrow and get all of the records and get in touch with all of buyers who dealt with you. In the interest of full disclosure, I took the liberty of making the sales I made, look like they came through me. The other records can always be tweaked as needed."

Sergio cleared his throat. "I can help with that."

His little sister shot him a grateful look.

Since that matter seemed to be settled, Ciana spoke next. "Can we now, please, tell her about Marks?"

Something about her sister-in-law's expression and tone when she said the named confused her. She looked over to her father.

A tempest crossed his face. "The man you know as Grant Marks is actually called Emilio De Luca." His hand clenched into a fist. "He was one of your kidnappers."

Her eyes widened with disbelief. "What?!"

Constantin nodded as he bit back a snarl. "The whole thing that finally set our reunion in motion was Cordula Loffredo, the woman who was your nanny, passing away a few weeks ago. She noticed you in town, got a glimpse of your birthmark and realized who you were. It wasn't until she was giving her last confession a couple months later, that she admitted to being a part of your kidnapping and named her accomplices-De Luca and Remigio Russo."

"But I've known Marks...De Luca...whatever his name is, for years! Does he know who I am? If that is the case, did he just recently figure it out or did he know the whole time??" The latter seemed much more likely to her. The chances of her just happening to eventually cross paths with one of her kidnappers was likely to be infinitesimally small, at least in her opinion.

Macario's face was full of malevolence. "We plan on asking him that exact question when he arrives here."

Valentino's grin was completely lacking in warmth. "The name change threw us for a bit, but my guys in the States finally located him. They'll be taking off with him any moment now. It's one of the benefits of having a private plane."

She looked around at her family. "I want a piece of him! I want a very, very large piece of him!" Having a name and a face to put on her lifelong agony, rather than some abstract person made her nearly foam at the mouth.

"Of course!" Esta replied. "But officially, on that day, you'll be joining us for our monthly sisters-in-law lunch for the first time. Our mothers watch the children and the men aren't allowed so they all get together to pass the time. Don't worry, we'll give you a full recap if it should ever be needed."

Natala took a turn to speak. "I'm hosting it this time. Come by as soon as you can, so you know what the house looks like. One of us can pick up an extra hostess gift for you to give to me."

"I can do that." Gina replied. She smiled at her husband's little sister. "I'll text you to let you know what I pick up. On second thought, I'll call you. And I'll remember to pay in cash. I'll pass on the receipt to you as soon as possible. Best not to leave a digital trail." Her husband could not have looked prouder.

"And I'll be giving you a ride out there." Paola grinned. "Since your driver doesn't start until after the weekend, you need someone to give you a lift. It's the least out of the way for me to come get you and drive out to Natala's."

The youngest Gismondi looked at each of her sisters-in-law in turn. They did not even share blood with her but they were doing their utmost to protect her and cover for her. Her heart swelled with gratitude. *"Grazie mille."*

"We're family." Ciana's voice was soft. "That man is one of the people responsible for making yours, our husbands' and our father-in-law's lives hell for near three decades. No thanks are needed."

When the women finished plotting the alibi, Valentino spoke again as he glanced around the room. "A couple of my other guys also told me that they think they're close to locating Samenson as well. Seems he went off the grid for a while, which explains the holdup."

She froze when she heard the name. For a moment, she felt like she was eight years old again, cowering down while a large fist slammed into her little body. Her eyes swung over to Dante. "You promised!"

Dante looked at her evenly. "And I've kept that promise."

"Don't be so hard on him, sorellina." Ignacio intervened. "He's telling the truth."

"Then how could you know?"

"Constantin, Ignacio, and I were just outside the kitchen and heard you and Dante talking. We didn't want to be rude and interrupt." Valentino's voice and expression held no shame.

Out of the corner of her eye, she saw her sisters-in-law exchange a dubious look. "And why exactly didn't you let me know you had heard?"

"Would you have made us promise the same thing?" Ignacio was completely unabashed.

"Yes!"

"Then there's your answer." Constantin supplied.

She turned to her father. "So, you know about that foster father?"

He nodded. "He can't get away with what he did to you."

One look in his eyes and she knew there was no changing his mind. It did not bother her in the least to realize that she was happy about it. She had tried to forget and move on, but now she was relishing that bastard getting a taste of his own medicine. No one had the right to hurt Agostino Gismondi's daughter and get away with it. Her voice was soft. "*Grazie,* Papà."

"I still say, you should have let me go over there myself." Valentino said to their father.

"Yes, but right now, we're trying to minimize your sister's connections to the US, not add to them." His tone made it clear it was the only reason he was not already on a plane there.

Agostino's daughter quickly squeezed his hand. She was then struck with a thought and made a beeline for her purse, which sat in a corner. After a quick rummage around, she pulled out a passport, a residency card, an id card, a foreign driver's license, and a bank card, purposefully ignoring the name stamped on each one. "These need to be destroyed."

Constantin took the items from her. "I'll go out and take care of these, right now."

"Wait a minute." Valentino took the bank card from him and grinned, when he saw which bank it was. He pulled out his phone and made a call. "Hey, it's Valentino. Remember that favor you owe me? I need you to delete all records of this account. As a bonus, whatever money is in there, you can take for yourself." He read the numbers off. "It's done now? Good." He disconnected the call and handed the card over to Constantin. "Here you go."

While Valentino had been on the phone, Ignacio looked at the residency and id cards. He made a call as well. "Hey, it's your brother-in-law." His conversation mirrored Valentino's; numbers and deletions.

Constantin took the items back and headed out of the room.

Sergio held out a SIM card and memory card to her. "I took the liberty of getting this set up. Any pictures or the like in the phone that you want, let me know and I'll copy it for you. I have a friend on standby to erase any record of the old account if you want."

She nodded. "Do it now, please."

246

"One thing first though-what social media accounts are there?"

"They're all on the phone and they all have the same password." She quickly jotted it down.

Her brother gave it a glance, then looked at her again. "Later, we will discuss proper password techniques." Sergio was on his phone moments later. He then got to work on switching the cards, after his sister showed him what she wanted copied. It was all pictures of her family and all the messages from them she had gotten. The last thing he did was to snap the old SIM card in half.

Her hand rubbed her forehead as she wracked her brain trying to think of anything that might be missing.

Her father gently took hold of her hand. "Relax, *tesorino mio*. We will get everything taken care of."

"I want the door closed, once and for all. I can't be calm until that happens."

"There are only two links remaining. One is the landlords for the apartment and the gallery. Both are notorious for keeping horrible records. I'll make sure to call them and remind them of such. The second is the one who set up the residency papers. Do you know the name of the person?"

She shook her head. If Marks ... De Luca ... had told her she could not recall it.

"Then we will also question De Luca about that and will do whatever is required."

"Call the landlords now. Please, Papà."

Her father did just that.

She wanted nothing more than a fresh start. To not have to think about the pain, the agony, the loneliness from her first almost thirty years of life. Anything that could connect her to that she wanted severed, for once and for all. It was something she wanted to never be reminded of, ever again.

When her father finished the calls, she gave him a guilty look. "As I'm sure you knew all along, yes I do know how to drive, but I'd still like my driver."

His smile was tender, as he seemed to clearly understand the implications in her tone. "Then you shall get him, *tesorino mio*."

Constantin came back into the room. "Done."

His sister threw her arms around him. While there was still one thing left, her heart and her soul felt like they were shattering the bars on a cage of unworthiness that she had been trapped in since she could remember. It was the closet to having wings that she had ever felt in her life.

"Do you want to know how?" Constantin whispered in her ear.

"No."

"Good, because I wasn't going to tell you anyways."

His sister smiled as she planted a kiss on both of his cheeks and his forehead. "Get the children back in here. Please. I need them."

As every one of her nieces and nephews came into the room, she did the exact same thing that she had done with Constantin, and each instance made a special brand in her heart. The act made her feel like she had made a bond that could never be torn asunder. She may have been denied the joy of them from the beginning of their lives, but that would no longer be the case.

When the youngest two had woken and she had done the same, her father pulled her to the side and performed the same ritual. "You have nothing to worry about anymore, *tesorino mio*. I will do everything in my power to see to that."

She felt her heart and soul fly beyond the sky at his words.

The Severings

Her father's car came to a stop outside of a warehouse in the middle of nowhere.

Valentino's guys had arrived with Marks … De Luca in the middle of the night. She had only been persuaded to get some sleep, rather than waiting up, when her father promised her that she would get her chance to confront him.

When she was ready that morning, she called her father. Whether he had woken before her and just could not wait, or if he had ignored his own advice and stayed up the whole night, she neither knew nor cared.

"I will ask you one final time, *tesorino mio*, are you sure about this?"

She met her father's gaze and nodded her head.

He led the way with a gentle hand on her shoulder. As they got closer to the back, she noticed large plastic sheets had been laid on the floor, wrapped round the posts, and hung from the walls.

When her eyes landed on Marks … De Luca … she felt a rage she had never imagined knowing building up inside of her. He had been tied to a middle post, ropes around his shoulders, waist and ankles, and her brothers were milling around the general area.

Her father and her brothers had clearly gotten a head start on him. She found herself completely indifferent to his beaten state. Every bruise and cut upon his body were equivalent to a break in her heart, which had only recently begun to heal. Breaks which would have never occurred if it was not for him.

When their eyes met, she already knew the answer to the question she was about to ask.

"You have known exactly who I am the whole time, haven't you?" Her voice was dangerously soft.

He nodded, flinching slightly. "It was me who got your application pushed through at-" He groaned in pain as Ignacio cut him off with a well-placed kick.

"We told you earlier, there were certain words you were not to say!"

"Guess it slipped my mind." Marks … De Luca said through clenched teeth.

She could not believe the gall he had, giving them that sort of attitude after what he had put them through. Her gaze went from one of her brothers to the other and finally rested on her father. "What else have you found out from him?"

Her father's expression was even. "Only the name of the person who set up the papers. We thought it was only right that you be here for the other answers."

Marks … De Luca sneered at her. "You just couldn't have woken up a little earlier, could you?"

"Silence!" Her voice roared than dropped to a lethal low. "You will speak when spoken to. You will tell us everything. Is that understood?"

"Why? Why would I do that? We all know I'm not getting out of here alive!"

"Papà?" Her voice was saccharine.

"Yes, *tesorino mio*?"

"If I should decide that he gets out of this with his life, would you comply?"

"Of course, *tesorino mio*."

"See? There's your motivation. You have a chance."

Mark's … De Luca's eyes locked with hers for several long seconds while he contemplated. "What do you want to know?"

"Why did you do it?"

"I've always struggled with gambling for as long as I could remember. I loved figuring out the odds, loved raising the stakes, loved the thrill when the risk paid off. There was a period, though, that I made a series of bad calls, and I got myself in a hole that I couldn't get out of. I needed cash, and I needed a new start somewhere with a new identity. When I was contacted about a job that would give me both, I took it."

Her hand clenched into a fist at being referred to as a "job". "And you weren't the least bit bothered by the fact that you would be shattering the hearts of many people?"

"I didn't know any of you. Tragedies happen to people every day all over the world. If it wasn't me, it would have been somebody else."

"Did Russo have the same sentiments?"

"Pretty much. Gambling hadn't been his issue, but he had crossed the wrong person and needed out."

"Where is he now?"

"Dead."

"How?"

"About ten years ago, he fell for some bitch, and they got married. They had a few brats, the last one being a girl. He started to get a conscious over what we had done and started drinking to cope. When he drank, he ran his mouth. One night he ran it too much. He told me he was going to turn himself in and make a full confession and name me in it. I couldn't let that happen."

While she pitied Russo's wife and children; after all it was not their fault they loved such a man, Russo was one who had been directly responsible for her family's suffering, so her sympathy for them was not as great as it would have once been. Her next question was only to highlight what a despicable man Marks… De Luca truly was.

"So, you robbed a woman and children of their husband and father?" The disgust of his casualness over the whole thing combined with the thought that she could have found her way home sooner, made her blood boil, but she made herself not lose control. Especially because he was their only source for answers.

"Again, it happens every day. My interests took precedent to theirs."

"Who hired you?"

"Your mother's family … they were the ones who hired us."

Her eyes widened and she froze in place, as she processed what she had just heard. Sergio, Constantin and Macario were in her line of sight and she was sure her own expression was identical to theirs. She did not need to see the rest of her brothers or her father to know that Marks … De Luca had just gotten their full attention.

"Why?" Her voice was more of a hiss.

"He," Marks … De Luca jerked his head towards her father, "made them lose their daughter. They wanted to make him lose his."

That made her believe that he was telling the truth. He would not have known that, if he had not heard it directly from them.

She felt sick to her stomach at the thought of sharing blood with people like those. No wonder her mother had made the choice that she did, when it was between her father and them. They had driven their own daughter away and still refused to take responsibility for it. Then, to punish her father in the worst possible way because of their actions. "Hold your tongue until I say otherwise."

One look at her father's expression confirmed her belief in what Marks … De Luca had said was right. The storm that raged in his eyes could barely be contained.

While her head was still whirling from the revelation, she forced herself to push her torrent of emotions down, as there were still some questions that needed answers. "Loffredo. Why did she agree to be a part of it?"

"Loffredo was a distant cousin of your mother's. They wanted someone who wouldn't have last minute second thoughts. They figured the connection to your mother was far enough that your father wouldn't pick up on it. Her role was to set things up, so the job could be completed. After that, she was to stay around indefinitely and keep an eye on your family and give them monthly updates."

"Did they say to take me across the Atlantic, or was that your decision?"

"It was theirs. Your father's network is vast, not only in this country, but across the whole continent. They didn't want to chance him finding you so the other side of the ocean seemed like the best choice. Russo and I, we were supposed to drop you and forget you. Your mother's family had already set up a new identity for you. I decided though, to keep tabs on you. Every time you switched foster homes, I knew. When you started university, I knew. When you signed your first lease, I knew."

"Why?" Her tone was sharp.

"Simply put, you were my insurance policy."

She finally reached her breaking point with him and his abhorrent attitude. Before her brothers or father could react, the back of her right hand slammed into his cheek. It hurt like hell but she refused to let it show. In a way, it felt like getting a blow in for her mother, as well.

Marks ... De Luca turned his head to the side and spat a little blood out.

"So, after all this time, what made you decide to finally get me back to my family?"

"For a reason I did not know at the time, it seemed that I was falling out of favor with your mother's family. I figured I could win favor with you all by being the one to send you back. I didn't want to chance your mother's family finding out, though, so I thought just letting it happen was the best option. I didn't think it would take so long for your paths to cross. It's not exactly, like this town is a major metropolitan city! After I sent you here, I heard from a contact of your mother's family that Loffredo had fallen ill. When the diagnosis came back as terminal, she was convinced it was punishment for what we had done. Your mother's family got spooked, and figured it was only a matter of time until your father found out. What I didn't know, was about Loffredo selling us out!"

Her disgust with him, his indifference over what he had done and the damage he caused took over. She stepped back until she was standing on the edge of the plastic sheet. She waved her arm. "You all can have a turn with him."

He had opened his mouth to object but did not get the chance as Dante stepped forward and in one swift move, dislocated De Luca's wrist.

"What about, first, do no harm??" De Luca screamed.

Dante looked evenly at him. "First, it's a common misconception but that is not actually part of the Hippocratic oath. It's from another philosophical work of Hippocrates. For the second and most important, right now, I'm not a surgeon … I'm a brother, who was denied his little sister for near three decades. A brother, who worried about his sister day after day, week after week, year after year. A brother, whose sister suffered because of you."

She knew she had been right, when she thought Dante was at his most dangerous when he was quiet. She also knew that all of her brothers shared his sentiment.

While he was still groaning in pain from his wrist, Sergio picked up a piece of pipe, and swung it hard at her kidnapper's knee.

She understood the reason for his extra rage. Sergio would have never had his own demons if it had not been for De Luca.

Valentino's fist slammed into De Luca's jaw. The force from the blow made De Luca's head bang back onto the post.

Before De Luca could even have a slight chance to remotely recover in any way, shape, or form; Macario buried his fist into De Luca's stomach.

Ignacio decided to do what Sergio had done, only with the other knee.

258

Constantin pulled out a switch blade and slashed it across De Luca's chest.

Her guess was that Constantin did not make the knife go as deep into the skin as he could have. She was sure it was deep enough to hurt, but not deep enough to have things be over quickly for De Luca.

She was completely unperturbed by the screams that came from him. Each one echoed a scream her soul had screamed throughout her life.

When Constantin stepped to the side, her father took slow steps towards De Luca. A predator who had a trapped prey was the only way it could be described. In rapid succession, his foot crashed onto De Luca's groin several times.

"Papà."

Her father stopped immediately and turned towards her. "Yes, *tesorino mio*?"

"I'd like to go home now."

"Any special requests you have for how it's done, sorellina?"

"No, I trust you all to know the best way it should be handled."

De Luca's eyes widened as he realized what was going to happen. "Hey! You told me that if I told you everything, I'd get out with my life!"

Her face was completely cold. "You misunderstood. I simply asked my father if he'd comply, if I asked. I never said I would ask. I didn't lie when I said you had a chance. You ruined it yourself by showing what a vile person you truly are."

Every part of De Luca reeked of desperation. "You can't let them do this! You'll be just as guilty!! You have to stop them!"

Her eyes locked with De Luca's. "How can I stop them from doing something to someone I have never seen in my life?" In a swift move, she turned her back to him.

She only turned around when her father nodded that it was safe to do so. Her brothers had formed a wall, blocking De Luca from her view. Muted protests could be heard from behind them. She had no idea whom had gagged him nor did she care. She gifted them with a warm smile. *"Vi voglio bene."*

Macario spoke on her brothers' behalf. *"Anche noi ti vogliamo bene, sorellina."*

She gave them a meaningful look and made her exit, her father at her side.

They drove away from the place she had never set foot in, nor had ever heard of.

When they reached their home, her father helped her out of the car. He had to head out again, and she had made a point of not asking where he was going or how long he was going to be. Her father would be home again later. That was all that mattered.

She looked up at him with a loving smile.
"Ti voglio bene, Papà."

"Anch'io ti voglio bene, tesorino mio."

Lucia Gismondi walked into her home closed the door behind her.

###

Thanks for taking the time to read my book! If you enjoyed it, please leave a review at your favorite retailor.

All the best

J. B. Ingersen

About the author

The Light from the Dark is the first book by J.B. Ingersen.

More are in the works so keep an eye out!